A Little Blues Story from the Jersey Shore

A Novel by

Marjorie Duryea

ACKNOWLEDGMENTS

I'm indebted to many people for advice, encouragement, critique, editing and information. They include: Kera Voigtlander, Joann Lay, Mary Zikos, Ricky Villane, Chelsea Wilson, Eileen Speace and Jill Czumbil.

Discalimer: This is a work of fiction. Names, characters and incidents are products of the author's imagination or are used fictiously and are not to be construed as real. Any resemblance to actual events, organizations, or persons, living or dead, is purely coincidental.

For my Mother and Father and Ricky
who all in their own way inspired me to tell this story

2018

It amazes me sometimes when I realize I really do like Fran these days. When she developed dementia she started to treat me nice, so why wouldn't I? It took her losing her mind to like me—she doesn't know who I am—but I am grateful regardless. When she knew who I was she would always say I was lucky to have found Rocky and did I think I'd do any better.

"He's handsome and there's a roof over your head, what more do you want?"

Maybe she was right, maybe I have been the problem because I've wanted more. I am "spoiled and unrealistic and don't appreciate what I have." That's what the former Fran said, but since getting ill she has had a change of heart so I'm not so hard on myself anymore either. When she became my ally she started to say, "He's a bum, you could do better." I don't think he's a bum. I never found real proof of him cheating, and often wonder if my suspicions are more evidence of my own insecurities rather than his infidelity. One cannot take seriously what Fran says these days anyway—bum today, hero tomorrow.

When she told me Rocky was fooling around with another woman she couldn't be convinced she was wrong even after Angelina kept saying, "Ma, it was me, your daughter, Angelina," for ten minutes. I had a dentist appointment the day Angelina gave Rocky a ride to work when his car wouldn't start. Instead of being thanked, Fran accused her daughter of being a homewrecker; an act of kindness was what started Fran's negative feelings towards her children. She doesn't even know who Angelina is though so that shouldn't count and she likes me now, which I suppose should not count either. Nonetheless, it does make living with her easier and even though she is pouring milk on the cactus plant again it is only mildly irritating.

"Ma, stop watering the plant, it doesn't need anymore water." That's right, it's easier to get into her delusion, instead of spending time yelling about spilt milk, trying to get her out of her perceptions of reality.

"Okay, but why are you calling me ma, Aggie?"

"I'm Liz, not Aggie." I try at least once; unlike Angelina who never stops, desperately trying to get love and recognition from her mother; I am simply checking something from time to time.

"No, you're not, silly." She's laughing at me but willingly handing over the carton of milk with an impish smile on her face. A connection between lack of recognition and degree of affection increasing confirmed again.

Rocky's mother moved in with us six years ago because she was beginning to have some issues with leaving the burner jets on and locking herself out of her house on a weekly basis. Although she had not been diagnosed with any malady when the paper towels caught on fire twice in one week, Rocky said she really should move out of her house.

"What does she need a big house all by herself for now anyway, right?" The question wasn't directed to me since most of the talk was between Rocky and Angelina, or that's how I remember it. I did agree selling the house in Bradley Beach was a good idea; she didn't need anything so big since her children were grown and Leo, my father-in-law, had been dead for two years. But I never agreed that she should move into our house; at one point Rocky suggested Fran stay half the time with Angelina and the other with us—that was frightening enough. He said splitting the time was good because none of the grandchildren would feel slighted. Was that a real consideration? Fran was a typical doting grandmother but nothing extraordinary, although I did feel she favored Angelina's children over ours. True, I wasn't the most objective person since Fran was so abusive to me—but nobody was asking for my opinion either.

"There is no discussion here," Angelina kept saying, "that's why you have the big house and we have a small condo."

I didn't know what she meant by "that's why you have the big house" yet, but I did know her condo was quite large. Leo had helped them out when they bought it and they didn't have a mortgage like we did. It was true, Rocky's salary as a trooper was more than Tom's income as a manager of a restaurant, and adding a person to one's household raises expenses in general; her argument that her children were smaller and needed more of her attention annoyed me a little though—my children were young as well. They were only nine but I do remember saying to a friend, "well, I don't even keep paper towels near the stove top and Rocky doesn't know it but I hide an extra house key under a rock."

A lot of attention probably would not be necessary, so I didn't say a word to Rocky or Angelina. Also, when they discussed how our house was closer to hers so she could still go to places that she knew and see her friends more easily, I agreed. Or I think I did, it was more like an out of body experience, or a-deer-in-the-headlights moment. I did have my chances too—unlike deer that eventually move, I didn't. Not even to suggest an assisted living residence; she certainly would not have had any money issues after she sold her beach property house. That thought didn't come to me until a year later when she was entrenched into her evil mother-in-law role: when she was still cognizant of who I was and who I was not, namely her beloved Jaime. The woman who she had hoped would be her daughter-in-law someday—then I had to come along and mess up the plan.

2001

I am compromising, I accepted the position teaching vocals at the performing arts vo-tech for September. It is only part-time so I can still pursue my real goal of having a career as a singer while I help sixteen year olds follow the same dream. "Oh, please God don't let them make it before me." It's not that I wish anyone bad luck but it would be a little humiliating if they actually achieved their dreams before me. I have to be positive though, the vo-tech job is better than subbing and I am still singing with Gary's band. He told me he had gigs in clubs at the Jersey Shore when he offered me the job; unfortunately, the reality is the clubs turned out to be dinky little bars. At least it's a singing job and I've been doing vocals for him for the past few months. That's why I decided to move here for the summer: sun and beach by day and doing singing gigs at night, why not? I don't like the beach and I spend most of my days now driving back and forth to NYC for my singing lessons and to hang out with Mitzy for starters.

Once I moved from my rented room in Hamilton to my rented room in Manasquan, the reality was we hardly ever had enough gigs as promised; my cash is running low and commuting to NY is expensive. I thought it would be a shorter commute on the train from here than from Hamilton but it takes twice as long. I started driving into the city and the cost of tolls and parking raised the money concerns. When Donny, who plays keyboard in the band, told me about the part-time teaching job at the performing arts high school, I applied. It's not going to start until the fall but at least it makes me less stressed about all the money I am spending now.

I never had any desire to teach so I had to be very creative answering questions at my interview to teach at vo-tech. I've only done subbing, which is babysitting with an educational theme. It's good for part-time money when you don't want to commit or sacrifice your real goals. That's why it scares me to take this teaching position; so I rationalize, "only one year, get some money, make contacts." What kind of contacts for the industry can I make with sixteen year olds?

If I am honest, I have to admit I was feeling low about myself when I applied to vo-tech, it wasn't only about money applying for the position; besides, I didn't even think I'd be hired. I do have a BA in music but it's not from a conservatory, just a Jersey state school. Apparently, vo-tech is not that selective because they hired me. It is only part-time, nonetheless, my fear is losing sight of what I truly want if I go through with this. I then remind myself—it pays a little more than subbing with less days required. It is a continual struggle all the time being tugged in different directions. Mitzy says it's because I am not committed to my art enough; maybe she is right.

I found out about the teaching job on the same night the audience at The Seagull was particularly unreceptive to me. I have a problem with some audiences because I resemble Cher. You might ask why is that a problem? If you are not a singer it isn't, and I actually used to be very flattered when people would tell me I resembled her. But there is an incongruity between my looks and my voice or maybe the fact is simply—I do not meet one's expectations. It began back in high school when I opened my mouth to sing and people expected me to sound like her; I think she is a contralto and I am a soprano. I am a good singer, don't get me wrong, many have said I am an excellent singer, but I do not sound like Cher. It was never an issue in college; it wasn't like my professors marked me down because I didn't have Cher's lower register. But in places like our band plays it definitely is a liability.

"Hey, baby, sing *If I Could Turn Back Time.*"

Even if Gary could transpose music it would not satisfy them. In these places, how much you sound like the band or singer you're covering determines how popular you are. The greatest compliment is: "You're good, you sound like"—whoever. Artistry doesn't exist and it's actually a liability if one pursues it.

I love singing blues and jazz; that's what I want to sing, having a full-time professional career. Gary occasionally does let me sing some of my choice songs during the gig; it's nice of him because it's not the kind of music these audiences want to hear. I do have to usually transpose the songs though which is a bummer—I can't do that well, and I need to pay someone to do it. Gary doesn't know how to transpose music—or so he says. But it's not his fault most jazz and blues songs would better suit Cher's voice than mine and I look like her and I'm a soprano. Maybe one of the teachers could transpose my sheet music at vo-tech. I am either trying to make myself happy about the teaching job, or again rationalizing a positive for taking it, since I never wanted to be a teacher.

1996

Today is the first day closer to my goal of being a successful professional jazz singer. I am graduating today. Okay, I am not graduating from Juilliard—I bombed at my audition because my throat closed up. I was really nervous or I didn't warm up enough. I don't know why it happened but it just did. They did ask me if I had another song to show them but I hadn't prepared anything else. Later at— the sorry we didn't pick you exit interview—they did say I had a beautiful instrument but they didn't think I made a good song selection. They also suggested I prepare more and I could audition again next year. That really distressed me more than not getting in because I did go over my audition song, again and again. So much so I often heard both parents and the housekeeper humming the melody. I may not have made an impression at Julliard but I infected the household with an earworm. Also, I didn't want to wait a year. I was on the waiting list for NYU too. The operative word here for both was wait. I didn't want to do that, I chose to go to a state school to major in music concentrating on voice. My father felt better about that.

"Develop your brain, not your vocal chords."

Although, as parents go, both he and my mother keep out of my way for as long as I can remember. I never doubted that they loved me and I always felt loved. But laissez faire style child raising was definitely their philosophy of choice and practice. I don't know if it was the same with Ronnie Jr., my brother, who is fifteen years my senior, but it was their way with me. I was an unplanned surprise just when my middle aged parents had been planning to start traveling more; that could have influenced their hands off approach. My parents did not try to influence my college choices, but appeared to be more pleased that I went to a school more known for graduating music teachers than jazz singers. Although it was a year after my audition when I found out Julliard was probably not the best fit for my career goals anyway. Regardless, no way was I going to teach—no matter where I got my diploma. I have been studying with my vocal teacher George in the city for the past four years since being rejected from Juilliard. Besides teaching, he also coaches and arranges for a number of name performers. He only takes students he thinks could have a professional career—so take that Juilliard.

After the ceremony my parents and I went out to eat. Ronnie and his wife Joann sent money and best wishes: they were in California at Joann's sister's wedding and could not make it to my graduation. Since Ronnie always felt more like a father figure to me growing up than a brother I was a little disappointed he was not at my graduation. When I was five I asked my mother why my friends didn't have two daddies like me; I thought Ronnie was my second daddy. She then told me that Ronnie was my brother and not to be saying he was my "daddy" to people, but he sure didn't look or act like the brothers of my friends. It was very confusing as a child but I could tell from my mother's reaction it was best not to talk about it anymore.

I didn't hold it against Ronnie choosing the wedding over my graduation however. I would have chosen the wedding celebration over my graduation as well. In fact, I tried to convince my parents for us to go. We had all been invited to the wedding, but they opted to see their youngest graduate. It made me feel special, but their choice might have been more about their surprise than parental love.

We finished our meal and father said, "Well, we were waiting for today to tell you our surprise, Lizzie." We were both smiling at one another and I could hardly wait for him to hand me keys to a new car as a graduation gift, which he gave to Ronnie Jr. I might add. I've been using my mother's car because I didn't have one so you can understand my surprise.

"Lizzie, we are putting the house up for sale, we bought a home in Florida."

Father went on to explain how he wanted to retire while he was still able to enjoy it. My face felt like it was frozen in a smile, like some frantic demented beauty contestant knowing she was not doing well—nevertheless, trying to impress the judges.

"What about me?" Was that really my voice? It sounded so small to my ears.

He then said there was no rush, in fact, it would probably take a little while to sell the house; they preferred someone be there to help when the house was being shown. Gee, thanks a lot dad—my father appeared clueless—my mother did seem to gage my feelings better. She explained that once the house was sold I could move to Florida and live with them. Rules were as long as there was one senior family member, anyone over nineteen years old could live in this senior community. Before I could even formulate "Oh, God, no, in my brain" my father intruded on my thoughts.

"No, Madge, that would not be a good idea. My philosophy is you raise your kids right and then you need to let them fly and they will be fine."

Ronnie lived in the parental home until he was thirty-one years old and then moved in with his then fiancee Joann. He had never been pushed out of the nest with no idea where he was going. I could have said that, but how far would it get me, and I didn't want my father to change his mind about me living in a senior community with them anyway. Before I could say anything though, he handed me keys for the garage and told me to make a copy for the realtor. They were actually leaving over the weekend. Going to Florida so soon and in late May—isn't it already getting too warm? Mother said I could keep her car, a gift; they really only needed one car anyway.

"People actually use golf carts to get around this community. Can you imagine that?"

Mother sounded really chirpy and expressed not one iota of empty nest syndrome. No, I never imagined. So much for feeling special and loved but I was not going to feel sorry for myself. In addition to my singing talent I have pretty thick skin. A trait George says is even more important than talent, if you hope to survive in the music business, or any part of show business for that matter. I complimented myself on having only a momentary twinge of self-pity and ordered another glass of white wine and chocolate mousse.

"Three glasses of wine, Lizzie? Make that one your last."

"It's only white wine, Mother."

She didn't say anything—just gave me that look of hers with the little shoulder shrug she uses when she doesn't like something I say or do. As I said she really is not an overbearing parent—but she is always very observant on how much any family member drinks. Apparently, her father had had a problem with alcohol. I never met him since he was long dead before I was born. She did not have to worry, I definitely was not going to follow my maternal grandfather's path. Although I vaguely remember my mother telling me her father had played the saxophone and also sang.

2002

Mitzy was drinking this huge chocolate milkshake. I knew later on she would feel guilty, complaining about her weight. She wasn't fat but according to her if she looked at a brownie she gained two pounds. I was one of those annoying people according to her who could eat whatever I liked. It is true, my five eight ectomorph frame never seems to expand no matter how many sweets or chips I eat. I only deprived myself once in my entire life when in junior year of high school I had a bad case of acne. After Dr. Gill put me on the pill it cleared up and I resumed eating whatever I wanted. Life's not fair, and I made a note to myself that when Mitzy started feeling guilty later I would be supportive. Or at least try to distract her.

Mitzy was looking all around the boards and kept saying, "Ah, huh, not even one besides me." I didn't know what she was talking about, so to clarify she said it just a little louder—it felt like a scream to me. I know people talk louder sometimes when there is a language barrier, but apparently it happens when there is a comprehension issue between people who share a language too.

"Do you see any black people, does this town have sundown laws?"

I noticed a few people looked at us when she said that but Mitzy insisted people had been looking at us before, "from the minute we arrived, girlfriend." The before I was unaware of, but now I felt like crawling under the boards and burying myself in the sand. I have no problem performing before any size audience; I love to sing for people whether it is a large or small group. But I really am kind of a private person and don't like emotional displays when not performing. Mitzy is always dramatic, with no separation between her performing life and private life.

She is always big which is funny since she is five feet tall. Once when we were both in front of a window which was set up high on a building I said, "Where are you Mitzy?" She wasn't tall enough to have a reflection in the glass but I could see myself just fine. She is never overlooked though—she always says what's on her mind anytime or place. So there is no surprise she would get attention now. I should be used to it since we have been best friends for the past four years, meeting at one of George's student showcases, and I did recover quickly from the unsolicited attention. After working at bars where the patrons really don't appreciate my work most of the time—I have developed strong concentration skills. Mitzy had my full attention.

She was right; there weren't any black people. Come to think of it I don't think I've seen many black people since I moved into this area of New Jersey. I had never noticed it before until she pointed it out though. I usually meet Mitzy in the city; why would I want her to come to a New Jersey suburb to hang out when there are so many things to do in New York? Mitzy came to New Jersey this time because Gary let me perform a few songs I chose last night. I really wanted feedback from someone whose opinion I respected. Gary is nice and he actually has a good voice, even though he sounds like different performers based on the cover he is singing; he absolutely has no desire to develop his own sound. He tells me that is my problem, wanting to develop an original voice, "You need to sound like the singers you cover, Liz." I needed Mitzy to come to the Jersey Shore—for support and feedback; to my surprise she wanted to stay over to hit the beach the next day. I know the ocean is a draw for a lot of people, Mitzy being one of them. I should not have been surprised she wanted to stay and that's why we were on the boards of Avon by the Sea for its night's festivities. They do not have a glitzy amusement type boardwalk: there's only one restaurant, a snack bar and a clothing novelty store. What was the appeal that would make Mitzy stay another evening at the Jersey Shore? A band was scheduled to play in front of the gazebo in the evening.

"If you see anybody official looking, where is the car again so we can get a quick get away? Oh, Liz, if you can see your face, I am only kidding."

I am one of those people who sometimes expresses what I'm thinking very clearly on my face but not always aware of doing it. It is not like I thought she was really fearing someone coming after her, not my feisty girlfriend, but what in hell were sundown laws? She explained how many towns throughout the country once had laws prohibiting blacks to stay after dark—sundown laws. "It was accommodating all the white people who had black servants during the day, of course."

"We are in New Jersey, Mitzy, not Alabama. I'm sure New Jersey never had sundown laws, and it's 2002. I think you're safe." I felt very superior I might add, only to be shot down by Mitzy telling me that New Jersey did have towns with sundown laws in its history. Not only that, she was sure there were some towns that had them in this area too. She also added even when laws were changed, sentiments didn't always change along with them. She was definitely more knowledgeable about black history than I was, she was probably right about the history, even if I didn't agree with sentiments not changing. And while the subject of sundown laws did not interest me, I have appreciated what I have learned from her about black jazz singers that I hadn't known before meeting her. But the sundown topic lost Mitzy's attention as well when the boards started to fill up with more guys.

"Look at all the hot yummy surfer boy oyster crackers." I followed Mitzy's gaze directed at two guys leaning on the railing. I have to agree with her, they looked like background in a surfer movie. "Hot" and "yummy"? That's subjective—Mitzy has a preference for dating white guys, but I didn't object to approaching them and we did end up spending the evening with them. We hung out on the boards listening to the band which unfortunately stopped at 9:00 pm. "Avon by the Sea is not a Saturday night in NYC," Mitzy pointed out. She felt like dancing too, and asked if there was any possibility of a place around there to go. To her surprise Ralphie, her guy—or at least the one she had told me to keep my hands off of before we ambled over to the railing—said there was a place to dance right across the street.

Mitzy really lucked out in the dancing. My guy couldn't move to save his life but he didn't seem concerned about it. I am not a great dancer either but at least I have a good sense of rhythm and timing. But he was a really pleasant nice guy and seemed to enjoy himself in spite of himself. Maybe his drinking three Long Island lemonades was affecting his rhythm as well as his disposition. Yes, three, I would be under the table at that point; in fear I was becoming my mother I dismissed the thought, focusing instead on his being cute and upright. People do have different alcohol tolerances after all. It was so crowded in this place it's not like anyone could really move drunk or not anyway. Also, you could not hear one another above the music; we didn't stay until the last call, thank God. Then Rocco, my designated date, suggested an all night diner where we could get coffee and something to eat. Sounded good to me so we followed them in my car.

"You don't look like a Rocco Bennetti."

"What does a Rocco Bennetti look like?" He looked very amused when he asked me.

"Well, not like you." And I was not clear why my statement was amusing.

"Haven't you met any Italians from Milan? Aren't you stereotyping?" How did he know what I meant? And if he was suggesting I was stereotyping, wasn't he as well? It was true though, if your name is "Rocco Bennetti," I envision a dark haired man with dark eyes and an olive complexion, not a blue-eyed blond with fair skin. I looked more Italian than him with my Jewish and Armenian heritage. But I was glad we did not pursue this thread after he told me he actually was only half Italian—he favored his German/Irish mother.

"Okay, Rocco."

"Call me Rocky, no one calls me Rocco except my aunts." We continued our first meeting gathering information stage while Mitzy and Raphie had their heads together sharing a soda, looking like they had already progressed several stages forward in their relationship. At least Ralphie was keeping Mitzy's mind off the chocolate milkshake.

Mitzy is one of those people who likes the idea of being in love. She also seems to need a guy in her life all the time even if she doesn't like them. One time she asked me to go with her on a date so the guy would be less likely to try to make a pass at her. I asked her why she was going out with him at all if she didn't like him very much. She said, "No way I'm not having a date on a Saturday night." I did get along better with her date than she did that night but he wasn't interested in me; too bad, I liked him, he was a jazz musician.

In spite of appearances, bets were Mitzy would never see Ralphie again. I liked Rocky but I was not looking to be in a relationship. Yet when he asked me for my phone number I gave it to him because I didn't have any friends in this area. It would be nice hanging out with him even if I didn't need to have a guy in my life.

♪ ♫ ♩ ♪ ♫ ♩ ♪ ♪ ♫ ♩

It was on our third date when it happened; I didn't open up about it with Mitzy for a few weeks. There have always been myths about being shot in the heart by Cupid and stories of love at first sight: Romeo was in love with Rosaline one day, saw Juliet the next and was in love. I thought they were only myths or just happened in stories: it was my third date with Rocky, and it was as though I was seeing him for the very first time. A bam, bam, physical feeling—not just in my mind—but running throughout my body.

"Right, Liz, that is lust, not love." Mitzy was patronizing me, the girl who was always in love? At least I stayed in love longer than a weekend.

"When have I ever said I was in love, Liz? Those are your words not mine. I know the difference between lust and love. I've fucked guys I didn't even like. You have to be in love to sleep with someone. You either don't know the difference between lust and love or saying it's love gives you permission to sleep with them so you won't be a bad girl." She was shaking her little head at me with a superior smile on her face, looking like she was lecturing a child. How dare she? It was the first time our different opinions were making me so defensive.

"That's not true. I don't think girls having sex are bad and I've slept with my boyfriends."

"Right, and you said you were in love with all of them if I remember correctly." Had I? Well, I guess I did but that was only puppy love in my past; it did not feel like this before and I was a grown woman now for heaven's sake—this was different and I told her so.

"Well, lust is lust, but there can be different degrees, as there are different levels of like. I like my Nana's collard greens, really like pizza, and I really, really like filet mignon. Different levels of like, different levels of lust." This was not lust, furthermore I now believed people could fall in love with someone at first sight and stay with them for the rest of their lives. I was quite adamant about it, but also asked myself why I was getting so upset with Mitzy. I wasn't quite sure why; Mitzy had an opinion about the reason for my heightened emotions and behavior.

"Sounds like you are trying to convince yourself, Liz. Get real—you have only known this guy for what, six weeks? You can't love someone after such a short time. He hasn't even shown you all of his warts yet. After you've seen them and still love him, only then—maybe it might be love. You have to be willing to die for them too, that is also my criteria for loving someone. Man, child or your pet dog. If you are not willing to die for them it is not love."

Is that true? My parents loved me, were they willing to die for me? Was I willing to die for them? I know people say that but how do you even know what you would do when the house is burning. Nobody knows if they would run back in to save a loved one until they're faced with the situation. And it wasn't true I haven't seen Rocky's warts. Okay, maybe not all, but he is a chain smoker and does have a drinking problem. Come to think about it, I have been putting my life in jeopardy with all the second hand smoke. I am willing to die for him; it is love.

2001

I finally found a room to rent in a house in Manasquan owned by a widow named Mrs. Murphy. I was starting to despair I wouldn't find one, and my teaching gig is starting in the fall. While the priority is stopping the commute to the shore for the band and now vo-tech, I have to admit I also can't stand my current roommates. I and three other girls rent rooms in an old house not far from the parental house. Two of my roommates are absolute slobs and one is a petty thief who sneaks into my room, steals my snacks and borrows my clothes without asking. I could keep living with the petty thief but no longer with the slobs. We share a communal kitchen but I have been eating sandwiches from the corner deli in my room for two weeks since I saw Debra washing the dirty kitty litter pan in the kitchen sink. I prayed to find another room to rent as soon as possible. Thank God, I found one and I am moving out this weekend.

One good thing about renting rooms in private homes is you can travel light. They usually are furnished—there's no need for furniture. My clothes, my sheet music, my CD's and boom box—one trip in my car and I am all set in my new home.

Some would be depressed to be renting rooms, but not me. Not only does it afford me freedom since I am not tied down to things, I also feel like I am sacrificing for my art. I know you can't compare rented rooms in suburban communities in New Jersey to a Paris garret or a studio in Alphabet City in the East Village, as Mitzy always points out. She also says if I were truly serious about my career I'd be in NY. I am serious: I continue to study with George; and I am working with the band; and I also perform in all of George's showcases where agents and producers attend; the only problem is the industry people are usually not looking for jazz singers. It is only a matter of time.

Mitzy has a problem with me being with George since 1992 as well. "What can you possibly still be learning from him, aren't you ready to move on?" Am I fooling myself? Some famous opera singers stay with their vocal coaches their entire lives. Mitzy just doesn't understand because she never took vocal lessons to be a professional singer. It was a hobby for her and she only did it for about a year. She should be able to make an analogy though since that is part of her trade. She is an assistant editor for a publishing company and aspires to be a full editor. She never explores other companies for positions, figuring it is going to happen sooner or later at her present job. Why is it okay for her and not me? Why is it that I am stuck and not moving on, but she can stay at the same company and it is a wise career strategy? I am meeting her in the city to celebrate my move this weekend. I hope she will really be happy for me and not give me a hard time for choosing to live at the Jersey Shore instead of NYC.

♪ ♫ ♩ ♪ ♫ ♩ ♪ ♫ ♩

I got to the city too early, it's one thing I hate about taking the train instead of driving. Not the time on the train where I usually read or listen to music, but not finding a schedule that works for me. I am either racing to my destination with only minutes to spare or hanging out trying to kill time; time to kill but not enough time to go to a museum or do something without spending money. If it's not cold or raining I can walk around or people watch though, so I don't mind the wait for Mitzy since it is an unseasonably warm April day.

The publishing company Mitzy works for is in the 50's on the west side. I often sit on the low stone wall that surrounds her building when I am waiting for her. There are some colorful denizens who walk by on a regular basis. There is an elderly woman I have seen a number of times who strolls slowly down the sidewalk wearing an open leather vest with her bare boobs swinging down to her waist. What amazes me even more, no one seems to notice her except me. When I told Mitzy that she said, "Well it's New York, people aren't shocked about those things, like in the suburbs." One thing about Mitzy is she always has to throw her digs at me about the suburbs. When I am having a good day, I think it is simply her way to get me to move to the city. When I am feeling more vulnerable and defensive, I think her suburbs shaming is her own issue about growing up in a suburb in Westchester, and maybe we should be shocked at some things?

The wait wasn't that long and we decided after some discussion to go down to Chelsea to a cute little restaurant that has salads and wraps at good prices. It's not far from Sweet Basil either. Sweet Basil jazz club is one of our favorite places and it's closing this month permanently to our dismay; we want to go there while we still can. We were waiting for our food and I was thinking about what George told me at my last lesson: how a performer needs to be realistic about their type.

"Isn't it funny that people looking at us would probably think you were the jazz singer and I was the editor?"

"What? You don't think a black woman looks intelligent and educated?" She was smiling when she said it but cats always look like they are smiling all the time too, even when they are torturing mice, and she looked like she was about to pounce on me.

"I didn't say that." She was beautiful and one of the smartest people I knew.

"I only meant if we were being cast in a movie you would probably be cast as the jazz singer and me the editor."

"I know, Liz." Okay, so why was she making an issue about it?

"Look, I don't know why I brought it up. It's not your problem since you are not wanting to be a professional performer anyway." I thought that would be the end of it but then she said, "Okay, if you say so," in this sing-songy voice, obviously still annoyed. Mitzy can be so combative at times for no reason at all when we are only having a conversation. She continued to act irritated with me until she started to eat the second part of her wrap. I did cut her a break, she probably had a very hard day at work.

I often wonder why I rented a room since I have been spending three nights or more at Rocky's townhouse. Of course, I did not know Rocky when I needed my room in Mrs. Murphy's house, and even though I spend so much time at his place, it's not like he's asked me to move in with him. My singing gigs are often closer to his place than my rented room in Manasquan; it's easier to crash there than going home when I finish. He doesn't seem to mind and I certainly don't; it's not only because I love being with him, he has a huge place and I have more freedom there than at Mrs. Murphy's. Also, he has a large wide screen television and even though I am not much of a TV watcher I enjoy watching from time to time. It is also embarrassing to admit, I like how it feels playing house—like we are a married couple. I'm like a silly schoolgirl writing our names in a heart on my book covers.

At least three times when Rocky left for work I was still in bed. He kissed me good-bye, telling me I didn't have to get up, but to put the alarm on and lock the door behind me when I left; you don't need a key to lock it. That's when I feel like we are "playing married." Big difference, a real wife would have keys, but I never let that discrepancy interfere with my fantasies. Do I think about marrying Rocky for real? No—not really, only when I am playing house. We haven't even reached a level where we have committed to dating exclusively. I have no desire to date more than one person at a time like Mitzy regardless, and I don't have the time even if I had the desire. I wonder how Rocky would either, working full-time, but I really don't know what his feelings are about monogamy. We haven't discussed it.

One morning about an hour after Rocky left for work, I was watching *Good Morning America* drinking my coffee when there was a phone call for him. It was a woman and it didn't sound like a courtesy call from some business. She said there was no message, she'd call later so I put it out of my mind. The next time the phone rang I didn't pick up, letting the answering machine get it. It sounded like the same woman who had called previously.

"Hi, Rocky, it's Jaime, give me a call."

I was pretty sure "Jaime" was the name of his ex-fiancee. Rocky and I have not agreed to date each other exclusively—but Jaime? If this was the same Jaime maybe he hasn't really gotten over her yet. They could just be friends now; but why is she calling him? I had to remind myself—it was none of my business.

Even when Rocky took a call very late when we were in bed and I could hear a woman crying over the phone, I kept reminding myself—it was not my business. I didn't put my pillow over my head, that would have been ridiculous, but I couldn't make out what she was saying anyway. Rocky told me it was someone he broke up with and "she wasn't getting the message." Rather than feeling threatened or jealous, I felt sorry for her; would it be me someday crying on the phone while Rocky told his current girlfriend I "wasn't getting the message?" I hoped never, so my fantasies were not about getting married, they were about getting a record contract or a good singing job. Not only because of a true desire for that, but to also try to maintain an independence from the whims of Rocky. I'm not suggesting Rocky is never a player in my fantasies. Rocky is often there as my supporting significant other in many—but not necessarily my husband, or even a boyfriend committed to me exclusively. I want to be independent of him, not act like a "lust zombie," as Mitzy calls me. I would be dishonest to say it isn't nice to get his support though.

It's nice to have someone say you're sexy, beautiful and talented all the time. Although it doesn't make me comfortable when Rocky is calling other women "dogs." More than facial characteristics he has a real problem with women who are heavy. When I say these kinds of disparaging remarks bother me he says he doesn't understand, "You don't know them, and I'm not saying anything about you." It doesn't lessen my discomfort; what if I suddenly gain a lot of weight? It's better to focus on the fact that when he says these things he is only with me, and the women he is bashing are never aware of what he is saying. I also rationalize: he usually is a little drunk, has less filters up, and is thinking aloud. Must one be held responsible for all of the despicable things one might think? To be honest, I have to admit the contrast between his disparages at other women and the admiration he pays me is a guilty pleasure. That's probably the real reason why I am so uncomfortable—it makes me feel even slimmer and more beautiful at their expense.

More important than kudos for my looks is how Rocky feels about my singing. He is one of the most supportive people I ever had in my life. When I am not in a metaphysical big bang explanation for my love, one major attraction is he's always telling me what a "great singer" I am—how I am "the most talented person" he ever met. Mitzy always responds, it's not like he has been hanging out with professional singers all his life. It isn't a dig at me though she thinks I am good, it's a dig at him because she doesn't like him. I do agree with her, when he has had too much to drink he over exaggerates me to his friends, or to anyone else who is around. He is sincere though, even if he doesn't realistically measure me against other singers of my calibre. Mitzy is right, there aren't many singers he can compare me with at the Jersey Shore. Her bias against the suburbs is showing again nonetheless when she talks like that to me.

"Anyone who is really good, present company excluded, girlfriend, is in NY or LA."

"Have you forgotten The Stone Pony, Mitzy? Right here at the Jersey Shore?"

"No, but the last I heard you weren't headlining there were you, Liz? Besides, the performers make it big somewhere else first, don't they?"

Oh, give it a rest, Mitzy. That's what I have to endure from my best friend, so it feels good to have Rocky so unabashedly enthusiastic about my singing. My parents were always supportive too but much more reserved than Rocky. They attended all of my high school performances with my mother always bringing me flowers; I had the lead for four years in the main stage musicals. My parents didn't seem to be surprised, or overly impressed by my getting the lead in the first musical as a freshman, which is unusual; the leads are usually given to deserving upperclassmen. But from the very first day Miss Reilly heard me audition she was planning all of her musicals with me in mind for the female lead. It didn't bring me a lot of accolades from fellow students the first year since they felt Carly, a senior who was expected to be picked, was cheated. Instead of admiration, I got a lot of hostility from many upperclassmen, and all of Carly's friends. Then as each year came and I was cast as Maria in *West Side Story*, Laurie in *Oklahoma* and Julie in *Carousel*, I was the bane of many of my fellow thespians. I am not saying I didn't have friends, I had a lot, but I wasn't friends with girls who were competing with me for roles. When I went to the audition for *Oklahoma*, a junior named Michelle was there to audition for the part of Laurie too; she got up and left when she saw me saying, "waste of time auditioning if she's here."

One would think I would have had a big head, right? The reason why I don't have one has a lot to do with my parents. My father fell asleep during the first musical, *Brigadoon*. During the intermission there were cast members laughing about the "old guy" in the front row sleeping. I only thought it was my father because he was a lot older than the other fathers and my mother told me they were going to try to get seats in the front. Later, I asked my father if he fell asleep. He said he was only resting his eyes from time to time but saw my performance, "you did a good job, Lizzie." But could I be sure he was even awake to see it?

My mother was totally beside herself about my hair in *West Side Story*. "I can't believe that they didn't style your hair." My mother was always complaining about my hair—

she definitely did not like my early Cher hairstyle look— long, straight, with a fringe low over my eyes. She didn't even mention my performance, and her final words on the show were, "they could have pinned it up, or at least gotten that hair out of your eyes."

My father's focus with the musical *Carousel* was how it was not one of his favorites. He knew that Miss Reilly had also been considering *The Music Man* so he kept asking me why she picked *Carousel*. I told him there was a senior who was a really good dancer; Miss Reilly wanted to use her as Billy Bigelow's daughter, featuring her in a dance scene. My father said he was disappointed—he really liked *The Music Man*.

When I played Laurie in *Oklahoma* my mother approved of my hair—I was wearing a wig. My father said "you did good" but his favorite thing about the musical was Ado Annie. "God, she was terrific, I'm going to see her on Broadway one day." Now, I am not being spiteful or whiney; Jennifer Mauro, who played Ado Annie, was a really good actress but her vocals were weak. She probably would never make it to Broadway and I wasn't jealous either. I didn't even want to be on Broadway, but I would have liked more admiration from my own father. I finally got the admiration for my singing I had been seeking my whole life—from Rocky.

♪ ♫ ♩ ♪ ♫ ♩ ♪ ♫ ♩

I am not going into the city to hang out with Mitzy very much because it's summer with more singing gigs here in the evenings. And in spite of Mitzy's disdain for suburbia she has been coming to the Jersey Shore because she is a beach bum, attributing it to her Carribean ancestry. She started flying to Florida with me a couple of years ago too; I visit my parents every February, they are an hour and a half from the ocean but walking distance from a manmade lake with a beachfront in central Florida. During the winter when it's freezing in the tri-state area, it's great to be there, even though the lake is not a draw for me. The fact that I sit here on the beach with her now, when it is hot and I don't like the sand or swimming in lakes or oceans, is a testament to my friendship with her. Her testament to friendship with me—she always wants to stay to hear me sing in the band in spite of the fact that Rocky is usually there; she can't stand him.

She usually gets here by noon; it's a good thing we can walk to the beach since there would be no parking places near the beachfront at that late hour in the summer. We stay until late afternoon but I usually walk back earlier than Mitzy to get ready for work that evening, leaving her looking like a beached starfish. I can't understand how she can lay there for hours under the hot sun without the benefit of an umbrella or a hat; I guess when you have darker skin you have more protection. I am glad she has been coming often this summer, even though it means beach days for me. I am her friend, I am not going to begrudge her fun at the beach. I like having her hear me sing with the band too; in spite of the friction between her and Rocky.

She hasn't liked him or Ralphie—that wasn't going to last regardless—since she found out they were "cops." To be more accurate they are NJ State troopers but anyone in law enforcement is a "cop" to Mitzy. She tells stories of her brother, cousins, and assorted friends who have been stopped and harassed by police, "just because they are black." I don't know if that is accurate or a biased opinion, but there is a difference between local police and state troopers; troopers are better trained and vetted more than local police—Mitzy doesn't agree with me. "Bullshit, they are all cut from the same cloth, even if they are black themselves." Sometimes it isn't worth arguing with her.

I personally have only had one experience with law enforcement, troopers in fact, and it is a positive one. The summer before my senior year in college my friend Marianne, who used to live in Minnesota, wanted to go on a road trip to Minneapolis in her Volkswagen beetle. We arrived there with no problems and visited her friends, but on our return we broke down. The car was a total loss but the guy who came to take us off the highway agreed not to charge us for the tow. The car was not worth fixing according to him, but the tires were almost new, so he said he'd keep them and any other parts worth salvaging in exchange for not charging us. I thought she might have been getting ripped off, but when you are stranded on the interstate maybe it was a good barter since she didn't have the money to fix the car. We did have money to get to Chicago and then home from there, but Marianne wanted to have an adventure; she wanted to hitchhike to Chicago. She was crazy and I had visions of serial killers and sex slave kidnappers, but she assured me it was safe—people hitched in the Midwest all the time. We were hitchhiking on the interstate for only about a half hour when we were picked up by state troopers. They said it was dangerous to be hitching on the interstate and took us to a motel for our safety, paid for it and left. That's the only part of the story I told Mitzy.

I didn't tell her how Marianne freaked out because she was sure they would come back to rape us. No fear of serial killers or kidnappers but she definitely had a fear of state troopers. I didn't get much sleep that night, not because I shared Marianne's fears, but she was up all night—crying and pushing desks and chairs against the door—as a barricade to keep them out of our room when they returned. Unfortunately, she did not do this all at one time; I would just start to doze off to be awakened over and over again by the sound of scraping furniture against a wall. Maybe she kept reassessing the strength of the barrier or it helped ease her anxiety to keep busy.

If I had told this to Mitzy she would have probably said—see I am not the only one who doesn't trust cops and she was a white girl too. They were trustworthy though, they did not come back to rape us, and the next morning I refused to continue this hitchhiking adventure: we got a cab to town, took the bus to Chicago, then flew back home. I will always thank those troopers, who may have averted actual harm coming our way, if we had continued to hitchhike. Don't stereotype "cops," Mitzy.

Most of the negative things Mitzy says and thinks about Rocky are not personal. She has an existing bias having nothing to do with the actual man. Nevertheless, she and he are constantly having toxic verbal matches where I am the unofficial referee. One might assume because of Mitzy's bias that she is the one who always starts these exchanges, but not always. I can see her point of view sometimes and then see Rocky's at another. They are always pushing each other's buttons. Your buttons can only be pushed if you allow them to be pushed; don't react. They also seem unable or unwilling to analyze moves. If you know what the reaction will be, don't instigate it either; I keep saying both to each of them to no avail. They put me figuratively, and literally in the middle of them sometimes on those rare occasions when we are all sitting on Rocky's couch or at a bar having a drink together after my set.

Rocky is not innocent of narrow-minded bias towards Mitzy either. He has accused her of being jealous of him because she really has the hots for me. He has said this absurdity more than once right to her face. Not only am I shocked, I have to question why some men when they meet women who do not like them react by calling them lesbians. Foul on Rocky. The trouble with being a referee in these verbal matches is all you can do is cry foul all the time. There is never a winner.

♪ ♫ ♩ ♪ ♫ ♩ ♪ ♫ ♩

The evening started out okay when we met up with Rocky, I told him about our nice day at the beach; I had enjoyed the sun and sand for a change and now it was a beautiful full moon balmy evening. Then he had to annoy Mitzy.

"Mitz, I would think you are tan enough, why are you always sunbathing?"

He resented that she was there but it's not like I am on a date with him. I'm working with the band and they are both there to see me. I didn't know why it was such an offensive thing to say though but Mitzy replied very sarcastically.

"Well, I am impressed that a cracker like you knows black people get tan, and we can even get sunburn too." I never knew black people could get sunburn, but I was not about to admit it and definitely not at that moment.

Rocky has a temper and I've seen him come close to fists with men. Having a short temper is pretty scary when you carry a gun. Luckily, he doesn't carry one when he is out with me in the bars, and he doesn't let people know what he does. According to him he is supposed to be carrying his gun all the time, to be ready to help if there is trouble. I told that to Mitzy, and she said, "Good, at least I don't have to worry about him shooting me." She will never let it rest, but as much as Mitzy and he do not get along, Rocky never loses his temper with her in any significant way; or with any other woman for that matter. Even with the grouchy waitress at the diner we frequent, who always spills our coffees in the saucers on purpose. I honestly don't think he feels threatened by women. He always seems to be more amused than truly angered by them; if he does respond at all it's with a sarcastic remark. Before he could say a word I asked him to get me a drink. My water bottle was in my bag; I didn't need a drink, I just wanted to separate them. I liked that they were both there for me but there is always more friction than support. It doesn't make it easier to perform either; it messes with your concentration.

"It was unnecessary to call him a 'cracker,' Mitzy."

"When you act like one, that's what I am going to call you." Did he act like one? Well, I was not going to get into this with her. I had to go over my songs in my head and try to focus because we were starting in ten minutes.

When my gig was over we found out that there was a problem with the train from Long Branch to NYC. Mitzy would have to wait until morning to go home. She wanted to stay overnight in my room with me again but I am not supposed to have overnight guests, even if they are female. We got away with it the first time, sneaking in at night and getting her out early in the morning, but I didn't want to take another chance—especially in the height of the summer season. Very few rooms were available to rent now and I might not even be able to get another place to live at all if Mrs. Murphy threw me out.

"You could always move in with your boo if you got thrown out."

I told her I would never ask him if I could move in with him—I liked my independence.

"And this is someone you are supposed to love, doesn't he love you too?"

The truth was I hadn't told him I loved him and was not planning to, nor asking him his feelings either. Mitzy sounded like she didn't care if I was thrown out of my rented room. It wasn't true though, she was only giving me a hard time about Rocky as usual.

Rocky was not privy to all our girl talk but was aware of the train and rented room issues. He told Mitzy she could stay in the spare bedroom in his townhouse. She replied,

"Excuse me." Then stormed off to the restroom: she banged her glass on the bartop before leaving and had an expression on her face like she just ate a lemon. One might think he had insulted her rather than offered a room. Foul on Mitzy.

"What's with her? Does she think she's not safe or I'm attracted to her? Yeah, right, like I'm going to leave you because I would rather be with her, or I'm gonna crash into her room and assault her when you fall asleep."

I suppose she might have been thinking such things. More likely, her thoughts were she might not be able to control her dislike for him, and she might do something rash herself. I didn't say that of course, but before I could say—she's probably only uncomfortable thinking she is intruding on us—he said: "Not my type, I don't go for ethnic."

What did he mean by "ethnic," did he mean black? Why didn't he just say that? I know Mitzy would call him a racist but I don't think someone is racist if they are not attracted to blacks.

Everyone has types that they are not attracted to as well as those that they are. I am absolutely not attracted to short men and I don't want to date them. Mitzy would probably say it is not the same thing, but I disagree. Short men are often mocked, bullied and marginalized which is disgraceful. That should not happen, but I still don't want to date them.

You can't control to whom you're attracted, and my bias began before my sexual preferences were even completely formed. In middle school I towered over all the boys in my class—they called me, "Lizard Lizzy." Not quite sure what the metaphorical value was—using a lizard for height—nevertheless, it paved the way for the development of my short men bias which I still have today. I didn't meet a datable boy who wasn't shorter than me until my boyfriend Kenny in sophomore year of high school. And even with Kenny I could only wear low heels to our junior prom. Today when I meet a guy who asks me out, before I say yes I ask: "is he tall enough so I can wear my high heels?" That's more important than what he does for a living or even his looks. Kenny was not a very good looking guy. He was very skinny and had a high forehead making him look like he was losing his hair at fifteen. His teeth were also so crooked, one tooth slightly overlapped another. He was from a big family, I guess they couldn't afford braces for all the kids. Even my mother used to say, "Well, he seems to be a nice boy even though he is not very attractive, Lizzie." He was tall enough, it was the only thing that mattered.

So I wasn't disturbed by Rocky's statement if he meant black. Saying he didn't go for an "ethnic" type did—George recently told me I was "an ethnic type." I am not completely sure what that means career-wise, or what it even says about me in general, but the fact that Rocky used those very words was very disturbing. I comforted myself thinking—he was talking about Mitzy, not me, so why worry about it.

Mitzy probably figured she didn't have a choice so we all ended up at Rocky's sitting on his couch watching a DVD eating chips and hummus. When he dropped some hummus on the rug and ground it in with his sneakered foot I was shocked. Rocky's townhouse was very tidy, definitely not a typical bachelor pad, and I never saw him do anything like that before. I think Mitzy was regretting her choice to stay and she told him he was "nasty." I couldn't disagree although I didn't say anything. To be honest, I was in disbelief that a man who lines up his shoes so perfectly in the closet and there isn't a speck of dust anywhere in his house would do such a thing. Rocky said that it didn't matter because he was shampooing the rugs the following week. He looked very puffed up when he said it though; perhaps he wanted Mitzy to think his action was "nasty," to push her buttons—getting her back for the earlier "excuse me." Let the games resume; foul on Rocky. Luckily it was already too late for many more exchanges and we all retired to our separate corners of the house. I only wish Mitzy and Rocky could get along better.

♪ ♫ ♩ ♪ ♫ ♩ ♪ ♫ ♩

In the summer we worked five or six nights a week; now we are lucky if we get one gig each weekend. It will pick up a little again during the holidays but this is the way it is until next summer. Gary is doing karaoke to keep generating some income and asks me to help. I only do it if he is in a real bind because it depresses me. The fact that he pays me a laughable fraction of what I get singing with his band doesn't disturb me; it is the sadness I feel to use my voice to fill in voids when the customers are not singing. I am used to encourage them to come up to sing themselves; I don't want to sing songs at the local bar when it's not meant to entertain. I am so ashamed of doing it I don't even tell George or Mitzy. It's even worse than teaching singing at vo-tech.

At least teaching I get a little more respect than doing karaoke. My mother is always asking, "Why don't you try to get a full-time contract at the school?" It's always said in a light tone, never sounding overly persuasive but she refuses to see I don't want to make a career out of teaching. I'm doing it only to pay for my singing lessons and other expenses so I am not forced to do karaoke to make money; I need to remind myself of that from time to time. I will admit, my teaching job is excellent money for part-time work. I am making more now too, since the other part-time vocal teacher left; I took over her classes. It's not so bad teaching the kids here either, I do like them. But I don't care how much I like my students or how much it pays, I'm at vo-tech only until I get a break.

♪ ♫ ♩ ♪ ♫ ♩ ♪ ♫ ♩

This fall is a little easier than last year because I have one year of teaching experience behind me. I was scared when I first started teaching because I did not have a clue what to do. Mitzy suggested I do what George does at my own lessons. It was helpful but my lessons and classes at vo-tech are very different. I take private lessons and I'm a motivated adult; I would be teaching twelve to fifteen im-mature teenage students in a group setting. A demographic not usually described as responsible or highly motivated. But Mitzy's comment did help me refocus my energy from anxiety to making lesson plans, based on my experiences with George. I mentally thank him every day for giving me a model of what a voice teacher does. My piano skills are better than last fall too after a school year of accompanying my students. I may even be able to play for myself in a piano bar or club now. I could not say that last fall.

I still don't know many of the teachers because I only see them briefly in the faculty room. The part-time people aren't required to attend the faculty meetings, and there aren't many opportunities to socialize with one another. There is also an unspoken hierarchy at vo-tech between full-time faculty and part-time staff. We aren't even called teachers; we are "consultants." It doesn't matter that we are teaching exactly the same as the full-time faculty. It is only a different label, but truthfully—we are not respected as "real teachers" by many. It does not bother me personally, I do not want to be identified as a teacher period. It would be nicer if there was a warmer atmosphere here however and less division. There's only one teacher I have become friendly with named Wylla. We even went out for coffee on our breaks a couple of times. The windowless break room becomes oppressive as soon as there's nice weather outside. That's when Wylla and I started to become friends sharing some personal information, besides reflections on shared students.

Not only does Wylla have an unusual name, she is also different from those patronizing full-time teachers; she doesn't have a negative attitude towards the part-time staff. I feel appreciated by her and respected as an equal. She seemed to be a really nice person in general, that's why I thought we could be friends outside of work. I was happy when she suggested we go to a bistro near the school before summer break. Then I saw another side of Wylla outside of work, her interchanges with the server amazed me. She complained rudely with this condescending tone: about the soup being too salty, the chicken too rubbery and the knife not sharp enough. It could be framed as simply being assertive by some; I agree, you can tell them when something is off with your experience or food. Don't act like the server is personally responsible for everything, or threaten to not leave a tip, though. I honestly was afraid the server was going to spit in our coffees and I have to admit, I hoped that she would spit in Wylla's. If Wylla turned her head I might try to do it myself. Since the logistics of that were tricky and admittedly wicked, I chose rather to leave a huge tip which pissed Wylla off—maybe more than me spitting in her coffee. I told her, "The waitress did her job even if the kitchen didn't." I also made the decision right there, I could not be friends with this person outside of work. I would like to make friends at the school but maybe it's a bad idea to get too close to people. I don't want to make it harder for myself to leave; friends can make it harder sometimes.

♪ ♫ ♩ ♪ ♫ ♩ ♪ ♫ ♩

Another reason it's easier teaching this fall compared to my first year teaching has nothing to do with having gained a year of experience or friends. Simply—it is not 2001, when the twin towers were attacked. Thankfully, I wasn't at school on the very day.

I was at the bank when the first tower was hit and I thought it was a plane that crashed by mistake. When the second tower was hit everyone knew it was a terrorist attack on the United States. My first thoughts went to Mitzy and George; Mitzy lives on Douglas Frederick Boulevard about as far as you can get from the financial district, and George lives in the 50's. But who knew if there wouldn't be another strike? Thankfully, they were safe and knew no one personally in the towers.

My mother called me that day from Florida as soon as she heard the news, "Oh, I am so sorry, I know how much you like New York."

She sounded like she was a resident from another country instead of Florida. Didn't she get it? It was an attack on the United States; an attack on New York is an attack on all of us. The last time I checked Florida was still part of the United States. Sometimes she baffles me, but in her defense, maybe she was more upset than how she sounded. She never loses her cool over most things. I don't think I have ever heard my mother raise her voice even when she is complaining about my lack of hair style or my father's occasional cigar. Both of which I know really irritate her, not to equate those minor irritations with emotions about the towers. That being said, nevertheless she is not a woman who gets very emotional over any happening regardless of severity. When I was twelve she told me how her grandparents from both sides of her family as well as aunts, uncles, and cousins were all killed in the holocaust. It was so sad and horrifying, but she sounded as cool as an historian or a professor lecturing a class.

After the initial shock of the attack was over I started obsessing about what I was going to say to my students. I did not have to teach until Thursday but that was in only two days; what should I say to them? I didn't even know them well at that point, we had only started school the previous week. What if one of them had lost a close relative, how does a teacher deal with that? We had been sent notices that if any faculty or student needed to take a leave of absence it would be excused; it was the only outreach from the school. Maybe they supported the full-time faculty more but I was at a loss of what my role should be returning to school. I was not seeing Rocky, he was on emergency call in case he was needed in New York at any moment; I had a lot of time to worry about this. I was glad I wasn't seeing him during this time though, and was in a room with only a radio for news and no television. At least I don't have horrific pictures frozen forever in my mind of people jumping out of the towers, only what I imagined from hearing it.

When I walked into my room on Thursday, Brian, one of my students, had a large pashmina scarf from a prop box wrapped around himself. He was strutting back and forth across the room but would stop from time to time to wave or blow a kiss to the other students in the class. The two other boys were whistling and catcalling; I had only three boys in this class out of a total of fifteen students. "If you count Brian," Robert, the full-time drama teacher, said one day in the break room and people laughed. It was mean, but I didn't call him out on it either so I was as complicit as those that had laughed. Brian was entertaining but it had nothing to do with his sexual orientation. I looked at my students: the boys continued to hoot and whistle, a couple of the girls were laughing at Brian, and the others were talking to each other or fixing their makeup or hair. Everyone in the room looked like the only existential threat they feared was losing the admiration or acceptance of their peers. I was glad it appeared, at least on the surface, that no one had been personally affected by the tragedy on Tuesday. I still thought I might start the class with a moment of silence, but decided not to—Brian was too hard an act to follow.

♪ ♫ ♩ ♪ ♫ ♩ ♪ ♫ ♩

Teaching twice as many classes this year as last made the time fly; we are heading into the holidays already. I'm still going into NY for my classes with George and meeting up with Mitzy afterwards as well. I am so busy I only have time to ask myself, "What the hell are you doing about your singing career," once or twice a week.

December makes six months of being with Rocky; Mitzy told me it is the "make or break," point for relationships. Do people actually do performance assessments at six months? I can't relate but then Mitzy cannot relate to my "pseudo-marriages" as she calls them. I am twenty-nine years old and not counting Rocky, I have had three serious boyfriends. We were monogamous, trusting and loving, and there wasn't a true break up with any of them. No fights, tears or recriminations; they all faded away without histrionics due to lack of proximity. There was no one to blame either except for Henry Ford maybe. I used to say that as a joke until too many people would ask, "Who is he?" or "Was your guy gay?" How fast a rumor could start apparently.

Kenny and I kept dating after high school; he didn't go to college like me, preferring to go to work. He was a mechanic's assistant in Hamilton and hoped to be a full-fledged one after a few months. In spite of our full-time schedules we were able to see each other quite often. But then he moved with his family to Durham, North Carolina, right before my sophomore year. They had family there, and one of Kenny's cousins, who was a mechanic, told Kenny he could get him a job. We pledged to keep writing, calling and visiting.

A year later I met Peter in my sociology class, and we were together until graduation when he went to California for his masters degree. He wanted to be an engineer and develop more climate friendly cars; he planned to return to New Jersey but he never did.

I thought my relationship with Dan would last since we shared a common interest in singing, having met him at one of George's showcases. Not only did I meet him at a showcase, I also sang with him because his partner who he was doing a duet with was a no-show. I knew *One Hand One Heart* because I had played Maria so I filled in for his partner. He was very grateful; he was able to still play Tony and soon we were dating partners. He aspired to be a Broadway performer and had a beautiful baritone voice. I never suspected he harbored any interest in cars. But after only going to one audition, where he was competing with hundreds of people all vying for the same part, decided show business was not for him. He moved back to Wisconsin to work in his father's car dealership.

With all three of them, when they first left there were many calls and letters with a gradual reduction until we only exchanged holiday cards. We no longer talked about visiting one another after a while either. This past Christmas I sent cards to all three of them, even to Kenny, who is married with a kid now. I heard from both Kenny and Dan, but not Peter. My card was returned to me as well. None of these relationships felt like breakups to me, though, more like expirations. And I never applied a make or break evaluation with any of them.

I was not aware of the six month "make or break" norm before Mitzy told me about it, but now I am evaluating my relationship with Rocky more today than in any time since we started dating. One thing that does bother me about our relationship is he never includes me in any parties his friends are hosting. I am not talking about stag parties either, people bring their spouses or dates to these parties. How do I know that? He tells me. Mitzy doesn't understand why I don't simply ask him why he doesn't take me. It sounds simple but also needy; it would be humiliating. Why do I even have to ask? We were grabbing a bite to eat at a diner one evening when his friend Marty saw us and came over to our table.

"Hey Rocky, my man, it was great to see you at Vincent and Sue's party. Liz, Rocky tells me you are a great singer. We really needed you when they brought out their karaoke player. Too bad you weren't there."

"Well, maybe next time." What I wanted to say was— yes, it is too bad, how come I wasn't there? And Rocky didn't say one word.

This subject is becoming paramount in my thoughts now because of the holiday season. I don't know if I'll be going to any holiday parties or even have a place to go on Christmas. It was never a big holiday in my house growing up. We always had a tree and exchanged presents, but my mother is Jewish, even though I didn't know she was until I was twelve years old. Her father had come to America by himself in the early 1930's and lost all of his family during the holocaust. It turned him against God and all religion. My mother didn't celebrate Christmas until she met my father, a first generation Armenian whose family were unable to find an Armenian Apostolic Church near Trenton; they joined the local Catholic church. Growing up we were those parishioners people mock because we only went to church on high holidays. My father could not be shamed though; he donated heavily to the church, even paying for a few stained glass windows and a pew. He may have not walked into the church often, but when he did, it was with his head held high.

We attended midnight mass every year on Christmas eve—it was also a ritual going out to dinner before church as our family tradition. One Christmas eve we ate at a restaurant outside of Princeton. Afterwards my father wanted to go to a church in Rocky Hill where a client of his said there was a beautiful Christmas eve service. It was a beautiful picturesque little white spiraled church, the kind you see on holiday cards. It started to snow when we got there and I felt like we were in a living snow globe; it was so beautiful. The only problem, it wasn't a Catholic church; I told my father but my parents didn't care.

As a child I helped Polina, the housekeeper, make holiday cookies, but we didn't decorate the house other than the tree, or count the days until Christmas in the Casperian household. It only means more to me today because not having a place to go this year is just so pathetically depressing.

I've been spending Christmas with Ronnie since my parents moved to Florida but he is going down to spend it with them this year. He said Joann wanted to do something different for the holidays and asked me to change my travel plans and come along. I said no because I hate flying during the holiday season, and already had my ticket booked to visit my parents in February like I do every year. I am also still hoping I will be doing something with Rocky.

Mitzy said I could come with her on Christmas to her parents' house in Yonkers. Mitzy's parents are very nice and always treat me well but I can't say the same for some of her other relatives. I attended a barbeque one summer at Mitzy's parents' where her Uncle Mel had a table set up in the backyard; he was making jerk chicken with his brand new grill. I went to Uncle Mel's table and was standing with my plate, soon feeling like an idiot. He was ignoring me completely, serving everyone else, not even making eye contact with me. I was just about to leave when Mitzy came over. I don't know when she became aware of what was going on but she said, "Uncle Mel, Liz was next, give her some food, please." The "please" was drawn out to pleeeze and she sounded really pissed off. I then got served but Uncle Mel did not even pretend to be contrite about overlooking me. Yet, if you hear Mitzy talk, only white people are racists. No thank you, I don't want to go to Yonkers either.

I finally asked Rocky what his plans were for Christmas and he told me he was going to work. He hadn't even been on the schedule but he volunteered so guys with families could take off. He was going to go over to his parents in the evening though.

"What are you doing, Liz?"

I tried to keep my voice from wavering; how pathetic I was. Why am I thinking this is really a relationship? It was the first time in my life my boyfriend didn't want to spend time with me on the holidays. Mitzy says because this is the first time in my life I am dating a "player." I asked her why she is always saying that; does she know for a fact he is dating other women? She said it's obvious the way he's checking other women out all the time, flirting with them right out in the open in front of me.

"If he is like that right in front of you, what is he like when you are not around? And you are the one who tells me he's always going to parties without you." She is right about the parties.

I told him I might go to NY on Christmas to see a Broadway show. "I haven't seen anything so I'm pretty open to whatever ticket I can get." I hoped I sounded as nonchalant as I was trying to sound.

"Well, I am not working the day before Christmas if you are free, we could spend the day together if you like."

I wanted to jump up and down and shout, waving my arms over my head. I slipped my hands under my thighs to keep me from moving. It felt physically painful to control myself, and I saw that my hands had red indentations from the chair seat when I finally felt calm enough to release them. I only felt happy for a brief time though, because I had the thought that he might have picked up I was about to cry before; was he only saying this now because he felt sorry for me? My question helped to rein in my enthusiasm like a tethered balloon. I was a mess; I needed to get a grip. I was never so emotional before in my entire life. Maybe I needed to get a physical? It felt like I had PMS all the time. I only had catastrophic health insurance so I did not go to doctors on a regular basis. That will be first on my New Year's resolutions list for 2003.

♪ ♫ ♩ ♪ ♫ ♩ ♪ ♫ ♩

George called me a week before Christmas to tell me he was moving to Las Vegas in March. He was going to work in a friend's cocktail lounge, leading a small band, and would like me to be the vocalist. It would be a combo of jazz, standards and popular music—but overall a lot of chances to sing the kinds of songs I liked. The money wouldn't be great but it would be a "living wage." You would have thought that I would have immediately answered, but I didn't. George picked up on my hesitation and said, "I understand it is a big move, there's apartment leases, storing furniture and other things to consider. And of course leaving family and friends." He didn't know I lived in a rented room with furniture that doesn't belong to me and I don't even have a plant. My parents are in Florida who I only see once or twice a year, and I could fly to Florida from Vegas just as easily as from New Jersey. It might cost more but my parents always paid for my tickets anyway so that wasn't even a factor. So why was it when this has been my dream since I was sixteen years old, I said, "Can I think about it and get back to you?"

I knew I would miss Mitzy, but we could talk on the phone and of course there would be visits; it wasn't Mitzy holding me back but leaving Rocky. What was this saying about me? I didn't have a problem leaving my best friend of many years but I couldn't leave a man I'd only known for six months? I didn't even know if he was dating me exclusively.

George said he was leaving for the holidays to visit his sister in Chicago; he'd be back January 15th, I could give him my answer when he returned. It should have been a no brainer for me, instead—it was making me question how serious I was about my art.

The fact I was torn about moving didn't mean I wasn't elated about being offered this opportunity, and the worst part was I couldn't mull this over with Mitzy. How could I? If I expressed doubts about accepting the job it would only confirm what she was always saying; and what I was thinking myself—I really wasn't serious about my career and I was throwing my chance away. And for Rocky Bennetti? Was I delusional?

I was meeting with Mitzy to exchange presents at her apartment. I so wanted to tell her, to at least share my joy, even if I didn't take the job. How could I share the joy without exposing my hesitancy? I could not bear to hear her condemnation.

I took my bottle of sherry out of my underwear drawer for a celebratory toast. I don't know why I keep the sherry in the drawer. Although, it did sometimes feel like I am living in a home for women run by some religious order but there are no rules against alcohol. Only rules concerning where alcohol imbibing can happen. I am not allowed to have alcohol in the living room where I am allowed to have guests, but since I am not allowed to have guests at all in my room there is no sharing of spirits with friends anywhere in Mrs. Murphy's house. That's why I am drinking sherry, wine feels more like a sharing experience to me. I don't mind sherry room temperature either and I like my wine chilled. I am allowed to use Mrs. Murphy's refrigerator but it's a pain going down there to get a bottle of wine then returning it. Especially if it is at night, she isn't too keen on seeing you walking around in your nightgown. She said no when I asked her if I could put a small refrigerator in my room. So here I am, drinking alone like an alcoholic on a Wednesday afternoon, watching dust bunnies dancing in the light. It is very peaceful though, I imagine myself in a little cocktail lounge sitting on a stool singing, *Mad About the Boy*. Lizzie the lounge lizard. Could it be possible?

♪ ♫ ♩ ♪ ♫ ♩ ♪ ♫ ♩

The day of the eve of Christmas will always be a sexual experience that will remain in my mind forever. Rocky and I made love all day long in positions I didn't even know were possible. I was sore and sticky but didn't care; it was animalistic. We would only stop to use the bathroom or bring some snacks to bed, and that was a treat because normally Rocky didn't allow food in bed. After hours of this Rocky and I took a bubble bath together; I thought it was the sexiest thing. Even if we broke up these would always be my memories in an x-rated *They Can't Take That Away from Me*. The only thing that ruined the evening was

I didn't spend the night with him. He asked me to go home because he was going to have to get up early to go to work the next day.

I wonder if guys know how women tell each other all about their sex lives. Mitzy says guys do it too but they are usually bragging about how great they were. I told her about us taking a bath together, thinking it was sexy and creative. She said it wasn't so creative, "Didn't you ever see that old Al Pacino movie with him taking a bath with his girlfriend? He's even a cop, I think." She said she thought it was *Serpico*. I don't know why it mattered but I went to my neighborhood video store to see if they had the movie. They didn't have it but they told me they could call their other store; it was an old movie though, they were not sure if they could get it. I decided to try the library and I got lucky. Sure enough—there was a bath scene with Serpico and his girlfriend, but it definitely was not a bubble bath.

♪ ♫ ♩ ♪ ♫ ♩ ♪ ♫ ♩

Rocky and I went to a club in Cherry Hill on New Year's Eve that had a dance floor with a large circular bar around it. It was very crowded and people scrambled to get seats, often losing them when they got up to dance. Leaving a coat on the back of a bar stool or unfinished drinks at the bar was no guarantee you would still have your seat when you returned from dancing. I was having a good time when this huge guy came over and said, "Hey, buddy, you're in our seats." We had been sitting there for at least a half hour because we hadn't been dancing, so I think the guy just forgot where he had been sitting. I never thought he was trying to get us to move because of the shortage of seats; Rocky thought otherwise though, refusing to move. He told the guy the seats were empty when we sat down and there weren't any glasses on the bar top, but the guy would not stop harassing us. It escalated to the point where the bartender told them to "take it outside." People say that in real life? What a surprise, I thought it was only a line in the movies. I was also surprised they were disruptive enough to be heard over loud music and lots of people talking. I told Rocky we should move but he refused and they went outside. I couldn't believe that they were really going to have a physical altercation over seats at the bar. The lady who was with this guy said to me, "You know, he is a Philly cop." I have to admit, I felt very superior to her when I smugly replied, "Well, you know, he is a NJ State trooper." It seemed like hours but in reality more like ten minutes when they returned. Instead of both being bloody and bruised they looked fine. They were laughing and had their arms around each other like they were the best of buddies. I never asked Rocky what exactly happened outside but apparently there was a truce of sorts. The rest of the evening was uneventful until the shouts, screams and whistles at midnight, and we stayed until they played Donna Summer singing *Last Dance*.

2003

It is the weekend following New Year's and I still haven't made a decision about the job. The fact that it's even something I have to keep weighing pros versus cons over makes me hate myself too. I still haven't told anyone either and have a palatable desire to share my dilemma with someone. Maybe if I could get reactions from other people it would help me to take the plunge one way or the other. I am definitely leaning towards turning it down because Rocky counts as a major con—times at least three. Yet, when I decide to refuse the job I never have the motivation to call George and leave a message, "I'm sorry, George, but I can't take the job, but thank you so, so much for thinking of me." Because when I lean pro to take the job, I'm filled with such happiness it's hard to give that feeling up.

I was in the happiness mode yearning to share it with someone when I decided to call my mother. Although, I didn't expect to get much enthusiasm from a woman who would be reading a book when I would run into the house yelling, "Mother, I got the lead in *West Side Story*," and she would look up from her book, smile and say, "That's nice, Lizzie," then immediately go back to her book. Her lack of enthusiasm or interest was the constant variable. It might be a different musical or she was engaged in a different activity but her reaction would always be the same. In spite of the response I expected, I called her and ignored the possibility she would probably burst my bubble.

The phone rang and rang. It was Saturday—they probably were out shopping or golfing or doing one of the many other activities they always seemed to be doing since moving to Florida. My father said he was busier now than when he was working and mother was his personal secretary. I am glad they are busy enjoying their retirement years, and I was about to hang up when my mother answered the phone.

"Lizzie, why are you calling, you just talked to us on New Year's Day?" I told her about the job and as many details that I had which I now realized for the first time were not that many—which she pointed out.

"Well, what does he mean by a "living wage"?"

"I really don't know, Mother."

"Don't you think you should find out before you go moving all the way across the country? I hope it is enough so you can at least get an apartment and stop renting rooms in people's houses."

My mother just turned one of my pros into a possible con. "Living wage" to me meant I wouldn't need to waitress on the side and I could support myself totally from my singing job. I hadn't even thought about my living arrangements; I didn't know my mother was such a room snob. It was the first time she had ever voiced any opinion at all about me living in rented rooms.

My mother has a strange relationship with the arts and artists. She worked really hard over the years raising money for local regional theaters and would weep real tears when she heard a singer like Pavarotti; who she says was kissed by the angels. Artists popular in what some would call the lower arts didn't get her respect, unless they made a lot of money. Of course she wouldn't say it like that, "I respect anyone who takes their skills and talents and can be successful." Related directly to the arts, she respected you even if she did not think you were a true artist or unique, as long as you were successful. My mother says Barbra Streisand "has a beautiful voice but there are probably hundreds of people who can sing as well or better." This is about someone she actually respects for her artistry too but even more for her business acumen. It is no surprise she thinks most people are being juvenile as well as unrealistic if they want to be a professional singer, actor or painter. She never said anything like that directly to me but she was a little bit too happy about my getting the teaching job at vo-tech for my liking. This became increasingly irritating, with her always gently pressing me to ask for a full-time contract. She stopped doing it this year; I suspect she thinks I have one since my schedule has doubled. Little does she know that she is mistaken. The truth is I now have two part-time positions not a full-time contract; I am not going to correct her. She is also a bit hypocritical in regard to aspiring artists when her daughter is teaching singing, which encourages the growth of more.

I ended the phone call adding "living wage" to the con list but keeping it on the pro as well because I needed to get more information to make a determination. I have to admit my mother is practical and is acting like an adult. Of course I need the numbers and information about the cost of living in Nevada. Although I bet my mother would be upset if she knew I have no problem with renting a room in someone's house again.

I wish I could talk to Mitzy but I know I can't control the hesitation from creeping into my voice. If she detected that I was even considering turning this job down because of Rocky she would freak out. I didn't need her to beat me up because I was doing that well enough by myself.

I know Rocky is the major con keeping me from taking this job but he is also one of the major enthusiasts for my singing. He doesn't know he's a con, so being one of my biggest supporters too, he would be a person who could appreciate the job offer. He might be able to help me make up my mind. Why shouldn't I share the news with him? I don't know what I was thinking—I couldn't wait to tell him.

♪ ♫ ♩ ♪ ♫ ♩ ♪ ♫ ♩

Rocky picked me up: we were going to a Mexican restaurant and then to see *Catch Me If You Can*, the new Leonardo DiCaprio movie. I told him my news right after we ordered our fried ice creams, I couldn't contain myself a minute more. He did react the way I had expected; he was thrilled for me.

"I am so happy for you, that's great. Maybe, I will be able to say, someday I knew that girl."

I was smiling with him and we even high-fived when it hit me like my face got slapped instead of my hand, stunned for a few seconds. Kind of like a slow reaction you get sometimes when you are drinking or smoking and you say, "I don't feel anything," and then bam. There hadn't been a trace of ambivalence or concern in his tone. Had I been clear that the job was in Nevada? Of course I had because he even talked about a vacation he took to Las Vegas a couple of years ago telling me how it had been one of his favorite vacations. There was no changing of facts—I had framed it clearly, our relationship would end due to this job but it was not a concern for him at all. Obviously we weren't in a serious relationship in his mind. It had only been me thinking our relationship meant more, and to think I had been so close to turning this job down. I have been an utter fool—but no more. I know this little romantic chapter in my life is ending but Rocky will never be getting a tearful call from me in the middle of the night. George says use every experience good and bad in your music because it all helps to give your performances depth and your song a true emotional underpinning. I can thank Rocky for breaking my heart and giving my songs more truth.

I was truly fine, and I enjoyed the rest of the evening too, but when he asked me to spend the night with him—I asked him to drop me off at my place because I was a little tired. I took satisfaction in that he looked surprised. Then he started begging me, sounding like a little kid pestering his mother for candy or a toy at a store.

"Oh, come on Liz, don't you want to celebrate getting your job?" I was no longer his plaything. He really was clueless but I had been right, he did help me to make up my mind about this job.

♪ ♫ ♩ ♪ ♫ ♩ ♪ ♫ ♩

Ever since George offered me the job I have felt lost. It felt like when I used to go sailing with my father on Casco Bay. Sometimes when it was very windy I lost sight of our destination because we were too busy tacking, making corrections so we wouldn't get tossed into the water. Forget about the destination, let's keep from tipping over, mates. Today for the first time it felt like clear sailing. I called George as soon as I thought it was not totally rude on a Sunday morning. I didn't know what Sunday meant to George or his sister. Was it a day of rest, a holy day or only reserved for family? Maybe it was one of those or all three because he didn't pick up and his mailbox was full; I couldn't leave a message. A mere breeze compared to the storm winds I have been navigating; I was not losing sight of my destination. I'd call him later today or tomorrow and I was free to finally call Mitzy.

Mitzy kept saying, "you go girl, you go girl, you go girl." Unlike Rocky, because she cared about our friendship, she also wished I was not leaving the area.

"Who is going to go out and play with me now? I don't even want to share a lot of the restaurants we've found with other people." I didn't want to dwell on cons today so I changed the subject to what we were going to do to keep connected. We agreed to call each other regularly every week but more if there was a need. We would only be a phone call away from one another. I reminded her too, that I was going to continue to visit my parents every winter, and she had a standing invitation there as usual. The only change would be we'd arrive in Florida on separate planes. If there was a will, we could keep this friendship going, even if it was long distance. I told her about this guy I knew who had a long distance marriage for sixteen years, and they were not even estranged. They only shared a home on the weekends, but what really surprised me was occasionally his wife would ask him to skip a weekend together when she was busy with friends. Perhaps, that's why they're still married, but I stressed the point to Mitzy: if a marriage could survive for sixteen years long distance, so could a friendship.

2012

Clearing out my mother-in-law's house made me realize how I had made my life so simple all those years renting furnished rooms. It's true when I was moving out of my parents' house I was upset about giving up my bedroom furniture which had been my birthday present one year. I didn't need it though because I was moving into a furnished room and had no desire to pay storage fees. I ended up giving it to Marianne because she was moving into an unfurnished apartment and had no money to buy furniture. Yes, my life definitely had been simpler without a lot of possessions.

Nevertheless, I did feel sorry for Fran being faced with losing so many of her things, even though she thought I was a witch who tricked her beautiful boy into marriage. She never let it pass every time I saw her to tell me how it had been a mistake when he had broken up with Jaime. Rocky told me Jaime was the one who had broken the engagement with him but that didn't seem to matter to Fran. Nor did it matter to her that they had broken up before I even met her son. This fantasy of hers was tolerable but the way she was friends with Jaime, socializing with her frequently was too bizarre. And her need to talk to me about her all the time was truly irritating.

Jaime visited my mother-in-law several times a week. I ran into her twice before I figured out that the white Sonata was her car. After that, if I saw one parked anywhere near Fran's house I postponed my stop, I was usually only dropping something off for Rocky anyway. I read once that being a physician could be a great part-time job for a woman once you got through the grueling training. You can work part-time, allowing more time for your family, but your salary is comparable to a full-time job for most people. Perhaps that's why Jaime seemed to have so much free time—she is a pediatrician. Fran talked about her being an award winning doctor all the time to me. But when I had my babies, was she also deliberately trying to be obtuse when she pressed me to use her as my pediatrician?

"She loves Rocky, and she would take care of his children like they were her own."

I asked Rocky, "Can't you say something to your mother?" He refused and said I was a big girl and I could speak up for myself; all I had to say was: "I found someone else." It was Leo who finally curbed his wife. Leo had been a real character, always making homophobic and racist remarks, but it had always been hard for me to think harshly about him for long. He would always take my side in many exchanges with Fran. I called him my macho teddy bear.

At the first family meal at Fran and Leo's house after we were married Leo made a toast. "To Lizzie, our newest member to the family, welcome, and forget all that Mr. Bennetti stuff, call me Dad, honey." I felt touched and also moved because he called me, "Lizzie." He must have heard my parents calling me "Lizzie" at the wedding since they are the only people who do. I don't know why but it made me feel even closer to him. My mother-in-law said I could call her "Fran." Leo bellowed out his objection, "Forget that, I'm Dad and she is Ma." Fran then said, not missing a beat, "Well, of course if you are comfortable, you can call me Ma." Comfort was never a factor for me—I had Leo's blessings; from that time on I called her "Ma." I also refuse to be withered by her look which reads—how dare you—every time I do. Rocky says it's only my imagination and maybe he's right. Only Fran and I know the truth; maybe Leo knew the truth as well and that's why he always had my back.

Rocky rented a huge dumpster and Angelina and Fran are going through stuff; separating things that are keepers from what is going into the dumpster. I help with whatever Angelina wants: I take things to the dumpster, pack stuff in the plastic storage containers, and run out for coffee and sandwiches. The problem is the dumpster hardly has anything in it and we are running out of storage boxes. One of the things Angelina does incorrectly is she picks something up saying, "Do you want this, Ma?" And of course Fran says "yes." She wants everything, even old report cards for Angelina and Rocky from grade school. Rocky says I should do more to help but he and Angelina need to be the ones who separate their mother from her things. I am going to continue to box and toss things only on their direction.

I finally lost it last night though when Rocky once again told me I wasn't helping Angelina very much. He said I could do a lot more to help his sister after another day of getting very little thrown out at Fran's house. I thought I did much more than other wives did in general since Fran is living with us.

"I let your mother move into our home in spite of the fact she is abusive to me and now you want to make it worse. You want me to be involved with throwing away her things and having her blame me?" I could not believe he said I should do more after now having Fran living in my house for the past three months. I had to admit though, I also took a perverse pleasure in watching Fran give Angelina a hard time instead of me. Nonetheless, it continued to bother me too how Rocky had never even asked me if it was okay for his mother to move in with us, making me finally blurt out, "Why did your mother move in with us anyway?"

"That was always the understanding with my father if there ever was a need. He gave us the full down payment for our house as a gift, it's the least we can do."

No wonder Angelina had said there was no discussion when they were talking about Fran selling her house that day and where she would be moving. Apparently, there had been a previous agreement she was supposed to be with us.

Hearing Rocky saying "us" and "we," one might presume I had been privy about this information when we bought our house. This was the first I knew about it though; I had always wondered how we were able to afford it. When we were looking at the house I also asked Rocky why we needed five bedrooms. I didn't know there was a long range family plan associated with it if Leo or Fran ever needed a place to live.

I don't know why I was surprised, we have been married for nine years but when it comes to finances we sometimes live more like roommates than a married couple. We don't have a joint checking account and we have separate credit cards; my card is the same one I had before I was married. Most of the bills Rocky has set up with automatic payments, and he'll hand me a check for the property taxes every quarter or will give me a roll of cash for food or for the boys. I take care of all of my personal expenses with my own money. My mother was shocked when she discovered that, "Why doesn't he give you money for your clothes and things that you need?" When I told her I never asked him she let out an incredulous gasp. "Why not? You are married, he's your husband." I thought at the time—he never asks me for money so he can buy his clothes—but I didn't say it because I knew my mother would chastise me for being sarcastic. But seriously, there is a double standard; at least he does provide for the boys and keeps a roof over my head. I am beginning to sound like Fran already and she has only been living with us for three months.

The paramount thing my mother finds appalling is that I don't even know what Rocky's salary is—when she discovered this she asked, "Don't you even look when you do your taxes?" Rocky does our taxes and I simply sign where he tells me but now my mother was making me wonder if I was a simpleton. I once read that most women of my mother's generation do not know anything about the family finances. She's more modern than I am, and atypical for her age. It is understandable though, she had been my father's book keeper; she married her boss. I never check our joint returns because I don't mistrust Rocky, at least in regard to our finances.

Every Christmas and for my birthday my mother gives me a huge check that covers all my personal expenses and then some. I really feel bad about taking it and told her she didn't have to give me money. She said as soon as I found out how much Rocky makes and opened a joint checking account she'd stop. I felt like a child being told to eat their vegetables if they want ice cream. The analogy is a little warped, however. In this case if I do as I'm told I won't get a treat. I still don't know Rocky's salary either, but I only cash the checks when I really need them.

Angelina called me after Rocky and I had our little blowup and said I didn't have to come to help the next day—someone else volunteered. I asked her who and she said a friend of mother's. She was being so evasive that I figured it was Jaime. I also didn't think any of my mother-in-law's octogenarian friends would volunteer to help clean out her house. It's okay with me though and Jaime can even invite Fran to move in with her if she wants; I won't object.

2003

I had planned to call George in the morning but when I woke up my full attention swung to how sick I felt. The room was spinning. My first thought was the mole sauce seemed a little off on Saturday; can one have a delayed reaction with food poisoning? But I didn't feel nauseous, just dizzy and it had been two days since I ate at the restaurant. I figured it was some kind of virus but it felt worse than taking two aspirins and going to bed.

I was going to call my doctor and hoped the dizziness would subside a bit because I would have to drive a distance to see him. Unfortunately, I still went to our family doctor who is in Lawrenceville; I would have to drive for over fifty minutes. I still hadn't found any doctors at the Jersey Shore; it usually wasn't a problem because I didn't go very often. I called and got an appointment for early afternoon the very same day. I knew I would be seen quickly because Dr. Rossi has been my doctor for my entire life. He isn't a clog in a corporation; sometimes he even answers his own phone. I probably would never change doctors in spite of the distance. He is like macaroni and cheese; he always makes me feel better even before he examines me or prescribes a single pill because he is so familiar.

The dizziness wasn't as bad driving and gratefully I made it to the doctor's without causing an accident on 195. After being probed, weighed and vitals recorded I awaited for Dr. Rossi's diagnosis. As I anticipated I felt comfortable just being in his care, secure with some embedded childhood faith that he would make it all better. He was writing something on his prescription pad and he said without looking up.

"Everything looks okay, Elizabeth, but I'm writing you a prescription for a really good multivitamin that you should start taking. It's common to feel like this in the early stages of pregnancy."

"What? I can't be pregnant, that's impossible, I'm on the pill."

"Well, according to your urine analysis you are pregnant."

"But I thought you were just testing for urinary infections with the urine sample?" Maybe he was looking at someone else's results by mistake. He then explained, along with checking for infections, with women of child bearing age he routinely tested for pregnancy.

"I wouldn't want to prescribe a medication not recommended for women who are pregnant, right?" He smiled and I had an urge to slap that smile right off his face. This was a mistake and I remembered my mother was told by a urologist once to never trust a reading showing an infection from a urine sample—they need to grow a culture to truly confirm its existence. Of course this was different, but maybe taking the pill since I was sixteen had affected my hormones, giving me false positives on pregnancy tests. I took the prescription for the vitamins but I had no intention of getting it filled. I also decided to get a new doctor.

I didn't think there was any point to buying home pregnancy kits, I would probably get the same results. Something was wrong with these birth control pills so I made an appointment with my gynecologist. The dizziness was probably from them too since it seemed that I did not have a virus. Maybe it was time to stop taking them. I did not want to get into a relationship anytime soon anyway. I was going to move to Nevada and concentrate on my singing career. I didn't want any men in my life for a long time.

When my gynecologist told me I was pregnant I still could not believe it. Getting pregnant on the pill was as unbelievable to me as the immaculate conception. My doctor said there was a 9% failure rate but it was more likely that I had forgotten to take it a couple of times. I wracked my brain as to when that could have happened. The only thing I remembered, one time when I was going to stay at Rocky's for a few days I took four pills out of the dial pack and put them in an empty medicine bottle. I was afraid of leaving the full pack at his house; how is that for irony?

The first person I called was my mother. I knew she would be very calm and she also is a regular earthmother when you are sick. Although pregnancy isn't sickness, it does not negate the fact I did feel sick about it. Growing up, all of my mother's maternal instincts seemed locked in reserve, not kicking out fully until you were sick. It was Polina who made my school lunches every day and baked cupcakes for my class when it was my birthday, but if I was sick Madge became mother bear. I faked being sick once when I was either in kindergarten or first grade; they called my mother and she came and picked me up at school. After I got home it was clear to her I had been faking illness, but to my mother's credit she stayed in earthmother mode. She knew I needed some extra nurturing that day. I needed it the day I discovered I was pregnant too.

My mother thought I was calling about the singing job again with the "salary figures" this time, spoken like the forever bookkeeper that she is, so she was a little surprised.

"Well, I thought you were on the pill. How did that happen, Lizzie?" I was so sick of asking myself the same question but was comforted knowing I'd only be asked it one more time when I called Mitzy. Rocky would never ask because I had no intention of telling him I was pregnant. It wasn't his concern; it was my responsibility and problem. I kept thinking that until I remembered how Mitzy was so freaked out when I had told her I was having sex with Rocky without a condom.

"I'm on the pill, Mitzy."

"Pregnant is not the only thing that you can get, girl-friend."

Rocky had told me he was clean because he was always being cleared at his mandatory check ups. But it is also true, if he had worn a condom I probably would not be pregnant, even if I had accidentally forgotten to take a pill; he is partly responsible. Nonetheless, I am not telling him.

My plan is to take the job and move to Nevada where I will have the baby. I will then give it up for adoption; I do not want to be a single unwed mother. I have nothing against single unwed mothers but I don't want to be one nor do I have any moral or religious views against abortion. I always thought if I accidently got pregnant I would have no problem having one. However, the very idea of aborting Rocky's baby is a choice I would never be able to live with for the rest of my life.

I keep fantasizing about finding a home for unwed mothers in Nevada near my singing gig; Mrs. Murphy's house has been good preparation, there would be very little culture shock and hiding my pregnancy from George would be easy to pull off wearing big tent-like dresses. George is gay, how closely does he look at women anyway? He'll probably never even notice I am pregnant. I'm not telling my mother about my plan so when she asked what I was going to do I told her I didn't know. She then asked me if I had told the "boy" yet.

"No, Mother, I did not tell the thirty-two year old 'boy' yet." She sounded like she was talking to an irresponsible sixteen year old me. I did make a mistake obviously but adults make mistakes too, don't they?

"Well, I'm not going to tell your father anything until you have decided what you are going to do. No use getting him all upset for nothing."

That sounded ominous, I didn't grow up in a family where I thought one would fear being shunned for an unwed pregnancy. The call was definitely unsettling, not very comforting: a marker entering uncharted waters.

Talking to Mitzy was not without its negative ripples either. The most disturbing thing was she accused me of forgetting the pills on purpose. To be more accurate, it had been my "subconscious mind in play." Her point was—I wanted to get pregnant and that hurt. She didn't get off it until I told her what I was planning and how I was not telling Rocky about the pregnancy.

"Getting an abortion is your body and your business, he doesn't need to know. But you can't go off to some unwed mothers facility and have a man's baby and not tell him. That's just not right."

I didn't want to tell him and I wouldn't have but Mitzy said she wouldn't speak to me again. Everything was all mixed up; now suddenly Mitzy was an advocate for Rocky?

I called Rocky after procrastinating about it for a couple of hours; I asked if he was free that evening offering to pick up a pizza. I figured the best way to tell him was directly, no hedging or eluding, just spit it out. I decided to do it after we ate the pizza. There was no point in ruining his meal and me wasting my money since I would not be able to eat the whole pie myself.

After I told him, for a split second before he spoke his eyes widened, and for the first time I noticed that his eyes were rather small—giving him a piggish look. I wondered why I never noticed it before, focusing only on their blueness instead. My mother had blue eyes and when I was little I always wished I had taken after her in that respect instead of favoring my father. I was pulled out of these thoughts when Rocky said, "What do you say, we can get married, okay?"

Did he say "married"? At first I thought I had imagined it but then he said, "It's about time I settle down, I guess."

Oh, my God, how had I so misjudged him? I had thought his happiness about my singing job was a lack of concern about me moving to Nevada; an indication of his not caring about me or our relationship. In reality, it had been a selfless act; he had not wanted to stand in my way.

That made me blurt out, "I love you." He didn't say anything but he took my hands in his, looking intently into my eyes. Then in a measured tone, as though he were talking to a young child and did not want to be misunderstood said, "I completely connect with you physically, intellectually and spiritually."

What he said was very moving, but somehow it didn't equal my three little words and I regretted having blurted out "I love you" like I had tourette syndrome.

My regret didn't temper me however and I said that it would be great if he could get a trooper job in Nevada near my singing gig. Maybe reciprocity existed for troopers like it did for school teachers between states, not even knowing if Nevada and New Jersey had reciprocity for teachers—but I was on a roll. Besides, Rocky could even change professions; he had a degree in business. He hadn't even wanted to be a trooper initially. He told me when he was in school he knew he did not want to go into his father's bakery business, but he also knew he wanted to be a businessman in some field. Ralphie was the one who wanted to be a trooper his whole life, he talked Rocky into taking the test with him as a lark. When Ralphie and Rocky both passed and Rocky found out what the salary and benefits were he thought—state troopers was a good business. Rocky let me keep talking and I thought he was in agreement with me until he told me I was "nuts," but not to worry it was only my hormones talking. It was the same with his sister Angelina when she was pregnant.

When I told Mitzy she said, "I told you to tell him you were having a baby, I didn't tell you to marry the guy." She asked me if that's what I really wanted to do. I lied and said yes. I didn't know what I wanted; things were happening too fast in my life. In a matter of days or even seconds my life was spinning like a wheel of chance on the boardwalk—got job, got pregnant, got engaged, lost job. It all seemed out of my control, would I like where it landed? I lied to Mitzy because it was easier than saying I don't know what I want and I am scared. I am more afraid now than before I told Rocky.

My mother said the baby was the hand of providence forcing me to settle down and be realistic about life; Mitzy said I may never be offered another chance to sing professionally again; George congratulated me wishing me "a blissful married life." He was surprised though because he hadn't even known I had a boyfriend. Whenever I talk to Rocky about my singing he says it should be put on the back burner for the time being; at least he still has me on the stove—I am only on a temporary hiatus with a voice I will be able to use in the near future.

Rocky used a cooking metaphor but he looks at me as a person remaining in play with a future in singing. His isn't script writing for a woman's role like the other people in my life, even George. It is 2003 not 1953; why can't a woman have a career and a family? I began to make a list of famous singers with children. Mitzy, never one to spare your feelings said, "First of all you don't even have a career yet. And those famous people have nannies and assistants to help out. Their kids get all fucked up anyway with drugs or they end up killing themselves though because their parents ultimately, when given the choice, choose their careers over the welfare of their children." That seemed to be a little cynical and it only helped to increase my anxiety like I was slowly being bricked up behind a wall.

Our culture says when you are in high school, "it's the best time of your life." This is when your hormones are out of whack with mood swings that change like the weather; a powerless being suspended between childhood and adulthood. So maybe expecting a baby, which is also supposed to be another natural high in life, is not as good as it is cracked up to be? Do other women, even those women who want a baby, feel confused and scared about the future like me? There is so much talk about postpartum depression but no focus at all on prepartum blues, and I can attest—they do exist.

♪ ♫ ♩ ♪ ♫ ♩ ♪ ♫ ♩

Starting this Sunday I will attend the Bennetti family meal at Rocky's parents' house at 3 pm. He told me to bring an appetite because it was a holiday meal every week. Always some kind of pasta, a meat dish, salad and desserts. When it was a true holiday there would also be Italian wedding soup, seven fishes on Christmas eve along with homemade cannoli and other pastries. Of course all the pastries were always homemade in a sense whenever served at the Bennetti's because they were made by Leo, Rocky's father, who owned a bakery in Asbury Park. The menu as described by Rocky seemed overwhelming. He also told me that they would be offended if I did not eat a lot. It was real pressure on me since in addition to dizziness I was now experiencing nausea. It would not make a good first impression on my future in-laws if I vomited at their table either; I was not going to gorge myself at a Sunday meal that sounded more like a banquet.

The Sunday family meal was a tradition in Rocky's family for as long as he could remember. Over the years faces would change with visiting relatives from the Bronx and upper state NY coming and going. And some would disappear entirely, like Rocky's grandparents, who are now deceased. One thing never changed though—anyone who attended was family or a very close friend. Leo did not like to let people he didn't know in the house. Growing up in the hood in the South Bronx, he didn't trust anyone, and he always thought people were going to steal from him. Rocky said he couldn't invite friends over to his house when he was a boy; he was only allowed to play in the backyard with them. If Leo was at work his mother sometimes let them in to use the bathroom, but most of Rocky's friends were so scared of Leo they would rather leave for home if nature called.

Leo was not a big man, but he had a big mouth. Rocky said he was more bark than bite and growing up he and his sister were more afraid of what Leo said he was going to do, not about what he actually did. Their fear was fed by his stories and their imaginations, not based on actual occurrences. Leo once told them how when he was a boy and reached across the dinner table to grab a roll their grandfather stabbed him with a fork drawing blood. He warned them if he ever saw them doing that he would do the same to them. But Rocky doesn't ever remember even being spanked by his father; his mother Fran was the parent who meted out the punishments not sparing the rod with Leo yelling at her, "Don't hit the face," and one never heard, "Wait until your father gets home," at the Bennetti house.

I grew up in a family that disapproved of spanking and always stopped eating before they felt stuffed; there was portion control in our house long before it was even a popular idea. These people sounded a bit Neanderthal so I was nervous about this meal. Leo didn't know me at all, would he even let me in the house? Rocky said not to worry, he had already cleared it. Honestly, that wasn't very reassuring—when I asked the question I was being facetious.

♪ ♫ ♩ ♪ ♫ ♩ ♪ ♫ ♩

Rocky set some ground rules before we went to his parents' house. One of them was we were not going to tell them we were getting married because he didn't want to give them a heart attack. He explained how he hadn't ever mentioned my name to them before so it would be too much of a shock. He planned on making the wedding announcement on the Sunday following Valentine's Day. True, it would be an appropriate theme for the week but we had been dating for seven months and he came to most of my singing gigs. Hadn't my name come up before at the Sunday afternoon family meal, even in a benign way? Didn't anyone ever ask him what he did Saturday night? I would obsess over questions like those in the middle of the night as well as over my belief that he would never have asked me to marry him if I wasn't pregnant; I truly didn't want someone to marry me out of obligation, and hoped he didn't think I skipped those pills on purpose.

Yes, I loved him, but I shouldn't marry him because it was not reciprocated. Mitzy said I shouldn't think like that; she thought better of Rocky now than she had before but she still thought he was a player. Whenever I brought up the unreciprocated worries she would say,

"He has to love you a little; guys like him don't marry a girl just because they say they're pregnant, but you were lucky you got pregnant first. Before some other girl did."

I don't call that luck and I sometimes imagine what would happen if I lost the baby. I was now in the weeks where there is the highest percentage of miscarriages. I didn't want that to happen but if it did—let it be before we got married on April 5th. I would toss and turn and my thoughts would not settle until I reminded myself I wasn't powerless; I did not have to marry Rocky. I could find one of those homes for unwed mothers and give the baby up for adoption. I wasn't sure whether they existed in 2003 and if they did, would they take a thirty year old woman? I couldn't answer that at 2 am when I couldn't fall asleep; but just thinking they might exist, providing me with a place to go of my own choosing, was always balm enough to quiet my mind enabling me to finally fall asleep.

The second ground rule concerned time. Rocky said his mother didn't like it when people arrived too early, the meal always started at 3:00 pm but if you were late it was a bigger gaffe. We arrived at Rocky's parents' house exactly at 2:50.

The outside of the house was lovely. It was an older two story frame house with a wrap-around porch; I felt like a realtor ticking off the pluses and "it is three houses from Ocean Avenue in Bradley Beach, walking distance to the beach." The front door was open and when we walked into the house I smelled something burning. Later, I real-ized it was cigarettes not burning food or electrical wiring when Rocky led me to the rear of the house. Rocky's father and brother-in-law, Tommy, were in front of the television, puffing away on cigarettes, watching some sports program. Rocky didn't say anything when his father yelled, "Hey, did anyone ever tell ya, you look like Cher?" Before I could reply Tommy said, "You're just looking at the hair, Dad, she definitely looks more like Sophia Loren." When Rocky's father began to protest Rocky said, "Her name is Liz and I will go introduce her to the ladies while you two battle it out who she looks like more—Cher or Sophia."

The kitchen was smokier than the TV room; Rocky's mother was the only one smoking but this room was much smaller than the back room with less ventilation. Mrs. Bennetti was working over a big pot of tomato sauce and was ladling out meat balls onto a heated serving dish; there was a big ash forming on the tip of her cigarette hanging precariously over the pot. As much as I was fixated on that ash, my fascination with Angelina drew my attention away from the cigarette. Rocky and Angelina did not look like siblings; they didn't look like they were related at all. Angelina was small and dark with thick brown hair and had a very large nose that drew my eyes to the center of her face. She looked like her father, and Mr. Bennetti, while not a handsome man, was attractive; that same face was not even slightly attractive on a girl. It's unfair how our culture objectifies women and I felt bad I was doing it. She might be a great person but I felt sorry for her. How had she felt growing up being an unattractive little sister with a cute blond blue-eyed jock older brother? It made me a little curious as well, how did Rocky have the nerve to call other women "dogs," with a sister who looked like Angelina?

While Angelina looked like her dad, I now saw how Rocky favored his mother. She was very fair with processed blonde hair but it was obvious she had been a true blonde at one time. I hoped that her coloring would be the only thing he favored because she looked like a dried up white raisin with a faceful of wrinkles. She looked very fragile as well; if someone bobbed her on the head she might crumble into a pile of bones. I hoped Rocky's face and five eleven frame would never be reduced to that of a wizened, bent over little old man. You start thinking about genetics when you are pregnant. Before I could give it more thought we were shooed out of the kitchen, told to find our seats in the dining room, and to call the other two from the back room.

There was enough food for twenty-five people and we were only six adults and a toddler in a high chair who kept throwing pieces of apple directly at me. I moved my plates closer to the edge of the table because he almost reached me twice. Every seating had a name plate with its own paper ashtray, and everyone lit up except me and Angelina even before the first course was served: a fruit cocktail with mini marshmallows. Thankfully no smoke was coming directly at me and the canned fruit cocktail was not a harbinger of the courses that followed. After a great salad and linguine with meatballs, which I mistakenly thought was the entire meal, Mrs. Bennetti and Angelina brought out a roast, mashed potatoes and peas with baby onions. Why were these people not obese? Tommy did have the beginnings of a little paunch but no one would say he was fat and Mr. and Mrs. Bennetti and Angelina actually looked too thin. Rocky was really buffed but I knew he worked at it, running or lifting weights everyday. I needed to get away from the smoke and give myself a little break from eating so I excused myself to go to the bathroom.

When I was in the hall I heard Mrs. Bennetti say, "She eats like a bird."

We were finishing up with the meat course when Mrs. Bennetti asked me what I did for a living and I told her I was a singer. Many people, when you say that around the Jersey Shore, never ask you where you sing or what kind of songs you sing; instead: "Oh, you want to be a singer." Mrs. Bennetti unfortunately was like many people. No, damn it, I am a singer; I only said it in my mind though but you would think that Rocky might tell her about my gigs himself. In fairness to both of us Mrs. Bennetti didn't give either one of us a chance to speak.

"Rocky was engaged to a lovely girl, Jaime, he probably told you about her. She is a doctor now. A girl with a real head on her shoulders." She kept talking about Jaime and I was waiting for Rocky to say something when suddenly Mr. Bennetti bellowed.

"For Christ's sake Fran, Liz doesn't want to hear about one of Rocky's ex girlfriends."

I was so grateful to him, and gave him a smile in spite of the fact that he was one of the most offensive sounding people I had ever met in my life. He was making anti-semitic, racist and homophobic remarks all afternoon. No matter what the subject he could insinuate one of his barbs. Right before Fran asked me what I did for a living Leo was telling me how all his brothers owned bakeries. His youngest brother moved from the South Bronx a couple of years ago to open up a bakery in upper state New York. Leo told me his youngest brother was always a whiner, and now he complained all the time about the "kikes."

"I told him it could be worse; at least he doesn't have to deal with the niggers like I do."

As soon as he said that, I felt Rocky tapping the top of my shoe with his foot; I guess it was a warning for me to be quiet. I was appalled but I wasn't brave enough to say anything; maybe my face communicated what I was thinking though because Mr. Bennetti said, "Oh, don't mind me Liz, I'm not a racist, I hate everybody."

For the last course they served espressos, coffee and a huge tray of assorted Italian butter cookies which were not Saturday's left overs from the bakery. Mr. Bennetti baked them fresh that morning but not at his bakery. His employees worked on Sundays so he was free to bake in his industrial oven in the garage. He had a lucrative hush hush business making birthday cakes, wedding cakes and cookies—cash only—pay in advance. Since the money was all tax free he could afford to give people good deals and word got around. But you did have to name the person who told you about him before you knocked on his garage door. It was like going to a speakeasy during prohibition but instead of booze it was pastry.

The cookies were delicious, so buttery they almost melted in your mouth. I could finally say an unreserved nice thing about Mr.Bennetti now—he was a great baker.

"Mr. Bennetti, these cookies are delicious, I've never tasted a better cookie in my life." Perhaps it was an exaggeration but they were very, very good. I also cut myself a break because I did have crazy hormones raging, heightening all of my senses these days.

"Oh, thank you honey, Fran can make a little box up for you to take home."

"Well, it's got to be a small one, Leo. Remember, I host my card club tomorrow."

I took three more cookies and put them on my plate because I had a hunch that Fran probably wasn't going to give me any to take home.

♪ ♫ ♩ ♪ ♫ ♩ ♪ ♫ ♩

Table talk was an art at the Bennetti's requiring a skill; after one month, I had not mastered it to participate successfully. There were always two or more conversations going simultaneously. Those skilled could bounce back and forth and participate in more than one. It was all noise to me and hard to follow. I would wait to be invited in when someone would say, "What do you think about that, Liz?" Of course my dilemma then was I often did not know what they were talking about, because I had been trying to focus on a different conversation.

A person could start a new thread with a provocative statement grabbing the table's full attention, and that's what happened when Rocky made the announcement we were going to get married. Everyone stopped talking and Fran started coughing, sounding as though she was choking. Then Angelina and Rocky started yelling, " Ma, Ma, are you okay, Ma?" And Leo, who was patting Fran on the back, was saying, "She's fine, she's fine, welcome to the family sweetie," which made Fran cough more violently. Tommy, who was looking at me directly, asked when we were getting married and I told him April 5th. That gave Fran the impetus to recover from her coughing spasm turning abruptly to me. Aging hasn't been kind to Fran, but when she smiled you could see in her youth she had been a pretty woman; she never smiled at me and now she was glowering. She looked like a gargoyle when she asked me, "What's the rush?" Why was she only looking directly at me as though Rocky wasn't any part of this decision? Fortunately, I did not have to answer, Leo rescued me once again from the claws of his wife and redirected the focus.

"It's about time if you ask me. He's in his thirties for Christ's sake. What—do you want him to wait til he's forty to settle down?"

It felt like Fran knew I was pregnant and that made me self-conscious. She wanted Rocky to settle down too, but not with me—with Jaime. All of those negative thoughts got kick started again—Rocky was only marrying me out of a sense of duty, not because he loved me. I did trap her son but I didn't do it intentionally; that didn't matter so I continued to suffer from the guilt of it.

♪ ♫ ♩ ♪ ♫ ♩ ♪ ♫ ♩

The worst thing about prepartum blues is it's overlooked because everyone is expected to be happy when they are anticipating the birth of a baby. I was expected to be doubly happy as well with the upcoming marriage according to my mother. She was going all out too: wanting a wedding dress, reception, flowers and a wedding party—the complete package. My mother has been on the phone since January calling from Florida looking for venues along the Jersey Shore. There didn't seem to be much chance of her finding a place for April so why waste my energy trying to discourage her? Rocky also wanted to have a reception asking, "What's a wedding without a party?" That was a real surprise but not as much as the shock when my mother told me she found a place. Not only did she find one, she got the mayor of this Jersey Shore town to officiate at the wedding. It was really going to happen, and in spite of my prepartum blues, my mother and Rocky's enthusiasm eventually began to infect me too. Even Mitzy agreed, "If they want to have a party why fight it? It's usually the highlight of most marriages anyway." In spite of her cynicism I asked her to be my maid of honor; Rocky got involved with the wedding party as well, making it expand beyond my comprehension.

Rocky started with Ralphie who was going to be his best man, then he wanted his sister Angelina to be in the wedding party; stopping finally, with two of his other buddies and their wives. I should feel reassured that Rocky is so involved; he almost seems happy. Perhaps his joy is not directly due to marrying me but there can be no denying that he definitely is excited about the reception. That's not fair though he even wants to go with me when I look for wedding dresses. He is not acting like a man who is being led to the altar with a shotgun at his back; I should be grateful.

I don't have enough time to order dresses so Mitzy and I have been going to bridal shops looking at dresses on the rack. My mother gently proposed, "You definitely should check out empire style dresses, Lizzie." She didn't have to suggest that style to me, I am aware of showing a little already and I will be three months pregnant in April. I don't want to worry about baby bumps on my wedding day.

Mitzy, Rocky and I are going to check out a bridal shop near Red Bank. It will be a full afternoon and evening: shopping for dresses; going to a trendy little restaurant; seeing a show at a local theater. I bought tickets for us to see a jazz quartet; it was a peace offering to Mitzy because she was annoyed that Rocky was with us.

"I thought the groom wasn't supposed to see the dress until the wedding." I told her we were keeping that tradition because we were going to agree on several dresses, but I would be the one to make the final choice. Rocky would not know what dress I chose until he saw it on the wedding day.

I had expected dresses with empire waist styles to look like sexless, shapeless sacks. To my surprise there were a few beautiful ones in my size that pushed up the bust making for a very sexy look as well as covering the stomach. There were also red cocktail dresses on the rack in the sizes of my bridesmaids. Mitzy looked beautiful in the dress but Rocky complained because they were red; he didn't think they looked right for a wedding. I told him how in some countries the bride wore red; he shot that down saying, "We are in the USA, Liz." In the end he did let me decide—it was too perfect to find the correct number of dresses on the rack in the right sizes for all the bridesmaids. Maybe there was a hand of providence intervention at play like my mother is always saying. Besides, Mitzy had been the only one I wanted in the wedding party originally and she liked the dress and looked great in it. My only reservation was a little guilt about Angelina; she wouldn't look good in this style because you needed a bust to pull it off. Alterations could be made perhaps but frankly, another style would not increase Angelina's attractiveness regardless. There wasn't any dress I had seen at any shop that would make Angelina look pretty.

By the time we finished with all of our activities heading for the theater, the temperature had dropped dramatically. Unfortunately, it was very hard to find parking close to the theater so Rocky parked in a "no parking" spot. He took a card out of the glove compartment and put it on the dash; he was about to get out of the car when Mitzy stopped him.

"What's that?" He took the card off the dash holding it by his right shoulder so she could see what was written on it, keeping his body and eyes front the whole time, never looking at her. Not to be deterred, Mitzy in response shouted at the back of his head.

"We are not here on police business. You shouldn't park here, Rocky."

Rocky then abruptly turned around to face Mitzy in the backseat and said, "Here's what I'm going to do Mitz, just for you. I will drive way up the street and let you out and then I'm going to come back and park here. Then when you get out of the theater tonight, you can walk way up the street again in the cold and I will pick you up there. Will that make you happy?"

They had a staring contest for a few seconds until Mitzy surrendered, but before she stormed out of the car and into the theater she yelled, "Abuse of power," right in Rocky's face. I didn't say anything; she was right, of course, we shouldn't be parking there but it wasn't like it was a handicap parking place or a fire zone. One positive thing, I picked my dresses today; Rocky and Mitzy didn't ever have to go shopping together again to help me find wedding dresses.

2017

I love when the light filters through the window in the late afternoon. I had a window that caught the western light in every rented room I lived in as well as my bedroom growing up. It has always been a quiet and meditative time for me. As a kid it was a daydreaming escape when I was sent to my room to work on my homework. Maybe that is why the ritual is so ingrained in me; rituals started in childhood are hard to break. As an adult I haven't been avoiding homework but rather wanting to settle my thoughts. A little glass of sherry and a little Miles Davis always helped too. Now I prefer herbal tea, but I still like to listen to jazz music and to get lost in my thoughts in the light of the room.

Lena Horne is singing *Stormy Weather*, the song Mitzy was singing in George's showcase when I first met her. It is a song I sing myself but it will always be attached to Mitzy for me. Her presentation was memorable at George's showcase for its rawness and truth. Maybe not technically above average but definitely a performance that got one's attention. She touched one's heart, any thought of vocal weaknesses were overshadowed, because she reached you on a visceral level. It took about three years before I could even listen or sing the song again after Mitzy no longer wanted to be my friend.

The worst thing about the breakup was I never knew for sure why it happened. I don't know if it would matter if I did, it wouldn't change anything. But not knowing what happened increased my grief. It makes me think of those poor parents who have a child who goes missing and the pain they have to endure; not only for the loss but also for the unknown factors. Knowing the worst outcome can at least release them from the limbo of not knowing what happened, as horrible as it is, even though it doesn't bring their child back. I knew it would not bring Mitzy back, but I continued to mull over all the things I thought might have brought about the split.

Mitzy and I went to my parents, as we had been doing for years, with the babies when they were around six months old. We were still talking and getting together immediately after our trip in February. It was around the start of spring that whenever I called she was never home, and she often didn't return my calls. When I eventually reached her she was always too busy to meet up with me. A new woman, Mary, had been hired as an editor at Mitzy's publishing company and Mitzy was spending a lot of time with her. Mary was a black woman a little older than Mitzy; when Mitzy talked about her at times she seemed almost infatuated with her. She told me Mary was the first person she could identify with at work. For some this would be a no brainer. She had a new friend—I was tempted to call and leave a song on her voicemail that I learned at camp when I was a kid. "Make new friends but keep the old, one is silver and the other gold." Yes, new friend Mary was the obvious reason why Mitzy drifted away from me, but other things happened before the split so I wasn't sure it was due to this new friendship.

There was the matter of her asking me how my "racist" father-in-law was and I said he was his usual bristly self, but he really wasn't a bad guy and I had grown to like him.

"How can you like a damn racist?"

"People do have flaws, Mitzy, human beings are not perfect."

I was going to remind her about her Uncle Mel who hated white people, as well as her mother's cousin Ruby who thought homosexuals were "abominations and deserved to burn in hell." But Mitzy looked sad, not angry, when she had asked me the question. It made me recall how Leo had treated her unkindly at the rehearsal dinner at his house. Looking back at it now I was insensitive to say I liked Leo; but I did, would denying it have changed anything? Probably not. I liked Leo because he was kind to me but he hadn't been kind to Mitzy. I overlooked her feelings about him and I hadn't stood up for her at the rehearsal dinner, both made me flawed.

I'll never know for sure if Leo played a part in the split; maybe Rocky was the cause. The only reason I thought that was he never asked, "Hey, where's Mitz these days?" Not even once; and right before the break he started to give me a hard time when I returned from NY one evening after seeing her. "Everytime you're with Mitzy you come back in a bad mood. What does she say about me? Bad mouthing me right, so you start complaining to me about your life." I suppose we did talk about him but I never knew what he meant about my "bad mood," and I wasn't the one who started to complain about anything that evening. I was just tired when I came back; I was not as young as I used to be. Walking all around, waiting for the train and the general brouhaha of NYC was more exhausting the older I got. I often wondered if he had ever answered the phone when she called: "Hey, stay away from my wife. Whenever she's with you she's in a bad mood, she is very impressionable." Of course even if he had done that it would not have stopped Mitzy from seeing or talking to me; you couldn't scare off Mitzy.

Losing her friendship left me grief stricken as though it were a death; it took three years before I could stop crying. She had been one of my closest friends, but I think what made it so hard to stop mourning was I had no one to talk to about it. I couldn't talk to Rocky because he never liked her. I didn't feel completely comfortable talking to my friend Sarah because I worried she'd think our friendship wasn't significant since I was so upset about Mitzy.

The only person I did talk with was my mother who shocked me when she said, "I am surprised it lasted as long as it did. I never saw what you two had in common."

Was that it, we really never had anything in common? No, Mother was wrong. Mitzy and I loved finding restaurants that only the locals knew in the different neighborhoods of Manhattan and Brooklyn. We loved going to hear jazz bands and vocalists and we went to practically every museum in NY—the Met was our favorite. More than anything else though we were cheerleaders for each other—when Mitzy was discouraged she'd never be a full time editor and when I was depressed lamenting I would never have a successful singing career.

Of course, we had our differences like all relationships. The one that bothered me the most was her view on music because it touched my life so directly. She didn't think white people should sing the blues because they hadn't suffered enough. She felt they couldn't truly identify with the music. I remember reading a biography of Janis Joplin and its author said she felt the same as Mitzy. That was the reason supposedly Joplin gave for why she started to drink and take drugs; she wanted to suffer so she could feel the music more. Reading the biography, I thought she didn't need to suffer more; she had pain to draw on using years of bullying and rejection from her peers throughout her school years. When the blues went mainstream the reason why all people were drawn to it was because pain is a part of the human condition. Everyone can identify with it; no race or ethnicity has a monopoly on pain.

Mitzy also felt that the early black jazz artists were robbed because whites took their music, made lots of money, and the artists were not given the recognition they deserved. That is the unfairness of art in general. There were painters who were forced to eat their paints to survive and died broke; after they were dead and gone their paintings sell for millions of dollars, fattening someone else's pocket. I don't know who is getting my money when I buy my sheet music, but I certainly am not getting rich singing the blues.

Even though she held these views she helped me pick songs and would compliment me on my renditions. Sometimes it felt like I was an honorary soul sister, more likely she was only giving me a pass to sing the music because I was her friend. She only refused to give me help or even feedback when I was singing at the Alcove on the sly. She lost respect for me because I was unable to tell Rocky what I was doing. I thought her not helping me at the time was patronizing. She shouldn't have been judging me, she was not familiar with the dynamics of marriage since she had never been married herself. Perhaps tension over that didn't help our relationship either.

Several years after the split, Rocky and I were at the Met looking at a Vermeer. Ever since he saw the movie *A Girl with the Pearl Earring*, Vermeer was one of his favorite painters. Our gaze was interrupted by a voice from the past.

"Hey, guys, hi. How are you doing?"

She looked the same, all smiles and confidence. I didn't return her greeting or smile. I remember there was a look of surprise on her face when I turned back to the painting without saying a word. I kept my eyes fixated on the milkmaid pouring milk from a jug while they chatted behind me, until I heard Mitzy say, "Well, it was great seeing you two, enjoy the paintings." I continued not to look back until Rocky said, "What the hell is wrong with you? Why didn't you talk to Mitzy? I thought you two were such great friends." That's the operative word—"were." Not speaking to her hadn't been revenge or anger on my part or even a reflection of negative feelings towards Mitzy. We weren't friends anymore but I still loved her. It was too painful to see her, and I have never seen her since.

2003

Angelina wants to give me a bridal shower against my wishes but she insists. The only friends I will have there are Mitzy and Marianne. All the other women invited are friends of Fran or the wives of Rocky's buddies; two of them are in the wedding party but I barely know any of them. I will be a stranger at my own wedding shower. Perhaps the shower is the way Angelina is getting back at me for her bridemaid's dress.

I was a little late arriving which was rude, since technically I was the guest of honor. It was Mitzy who kept telling me to hurry, "Can't be late for your own party." I had picked her up at the train station in Manasquan and by my own design was taking the slowest route to the restaurant; I was not looking forward to this. If I had been in control, I would have liked to celebrate by going out with two people only—Mitzy and Marianne.

When we got to the restaurant we were told that the shower party was upstairs. Now I felt a bit self-conscious about getting there late, I didn't want to make an entrance. But when we walked into the room nobody looked up; everyone was too busy drinking and eating antipasto. I was glad they hadn't waited for me and were enjoying themselves. The guest of honor was obviously not necessary to make this party a success which came as no surprise to me. Angelina came running over to us though and got everyone's attention in the room. She literally introduced me to the party guests since the majority hadn't even met me before. It was honestly too bizarre—it would get worse. She then took Mitzy and me to our table where Fran was seated with another woman around my age. That's the day I met Jaime, Rocky's ex-fiancee.

What was more absurd—the fact that Rocky's ex-fiancee was at my bridal shower and apparently had been invited to my wedding, or that she was seated at my table at the shower party? Fran was all smiles when she introduced me to Jaime, looking at my stomach the entire time. She has been doing that since Rocky announced our engagement in February. I sat down as quickly as possible so she would be forced to look at my face when she talked to me. I was wearing a big bulky sweater over leggings so I knew no one could see a baby bump, but regardless it made me uncomfortable when she talked to my stomach. It's like when men talked to my chest for an entire conversation, but that actually wasn't as unnerving as Fran talking to my stomach. I was tempted to order a white wine only to see her reaction. But with the way she smoked like it was the 1950's, maybe she didn't even know pregnant women are discouraged to drink these days.

Jaime did not look like I had pictured her, but no matter what she looked like in reality it would never be as good as what I had imagined. The real Jaime was in competition with her own overblown characterization that Fran had made, shaping the images in my mind. I always envisioned a tall woman who looked like a model with long hair pulled severely back from her face, wearing a whitecoat with a stethoscope hanging around her neck. She was always in medical garb in my imagination so seeing her in street clothes was mind blowing in itself. I always thought of her as blonde too but she had short light brown curly hair; and rather than tall and slender, she was short and a little chubby. Truthfully, she was cute; she even had freckles on her nose. She looked more like a kindergarten teacher than a pediatrician, maybe that is why she was so successful. One might ask why would anyone be threatened by this woman? Most wouldn't be but I was because she definitely was not an ethnic type.

♪ ♫ ♩ ♪ ♫ ♩ ♪ ♫ ♩

Mother secured the room where the wedding and reception would take place for a few hours on Friday night for a rehearsal; she is orchestrating every cultural wedding ritual whether I protest or not. For a life long hands off parent it seems out of character but it is related to the earthmother reserves she taps when I am sick. My dizziness has returned, worse now than previously, along with a lot of angst over this marriage.

The rehearsal practice, the marriage ceremony, the reception, and honeymoon all make me feel like I'm watching a movie about someone else getting married. It isn't a carefree chick flick either; this movie often makes me sick of heart. I never thought much about getting married throughout my life. I always assumed I just would, since that is the script for women in our culture and I had no objection to it. I never imagined though I might be marrying someone who did not want to marry me. Rocky has never even said once that he is having second thoughts, but sometimes I feel like a kid who was not invited to a party but finagled an invitation. I do get invited to the party but only because someone was forced or shamed into asking me; I don't want Rocky to be forced or shamed into this marriage. I feel ashamed myself sometimes though, thinking I'm taking the easy way. I then ask myself: is it Rocky being forced or is it me—due to my lack of courage to confront issues? Mitzy keeps asking me what I want for myself and to stop worrying about what other people want for me, "You don't marry someone because your parents want you to, you don't have to marry this guy you know." I am not doing it for my parents, I do love Rocky but even if I wanted to stop all of this right now it's out of control; the train seems to be moving too rapidly to jump off at this point.

♪ ♫ ♩ ♪ ♫ ♩ ♪ ♫ ♩

Fran and Leo want to host a little buffet after the rehearsal at their house. I was more surprised than thrilled about this and questioned Rocky how this was going to work knowing how Leo felt about strangers.

"How are they hosting a party if your father doesn't like people in the house?" Rocky said there are a few exceptions like his mother's monthly card club meeting. The ladies are allowed in only two rooms—where they are playing cards and the bathroom. Also, Fran uses paper plates and throw away utensils; apparently Leo is also a germaphobe. Rocky said that he imagined it would be the same kind of set up. It was still unclear why they were hosting a party. Rocky finally said I should feel complimented, "My dad likes you."

"Your father is baking the wedding cake and making cookies and pastries. He is doing enough."

"Stop complaining about them wanting to do something for you." I wasn't complaining and weren't they doing it for both of us? If it was up to me, what I really wanted was to chill after the rehearsal and I don't know what I did to get this admiration from Rocky's father. I barely say anything to Leo because I always feel intimidated by him. I'm glad Mitzy will be there with me; she is not intimidated by anyone. I was afraid she might want to be dropped off at her motel room after the rehearsal. She booked a motel reservation because she did not want to stay at Rocky's again, and my parents already sent their regrets because they want to go back to their room after the rehearsal. They are taking advantage of the venue's hotel services so for them it is an elevator ride up to their suite. Mother thinks of everything; I only wish she had booked me a room too.

The rehearsal went well, but I was very dizzy throughout so after we finished rehearsing I went up to my parents' suite to splash water on my face and lie down. Rocky stayed downstairs in the bar. My father, who still hadn't been told about the pregnancy, kept saying, "Butterflies, everybody has them before they get married, but it's usually the groom." My mother, knowing all, whispered to me: "Have you spoken to your obstetrician?" I told her I was scheduled for a sonogram when I got back from Key West. I wished Mitzy and I could crash here in my parents' suite for an hour. Rocky was drinking downstairs in the bar, so time was a priority however if we were going to get to his parents' house before he was bombed. Also, his parents and our wedding party were waiting for us.

We were the last to arrive at the Bennetti's. I was wondering how Leo would keep people in the designated rooms; would he have signs or theater ropes to keep people out of restricted areas? I was being mean but later didn't regret it. When we walked in everyone was sitting around with drinks in their hands, eating chips and other finger foods, but the buffet dishes on the back table were still all covered. Fran and Leo had prepared well for this party; but Leo had not been prepared for Mitzy. Hadn't anyone told him my maid of honor was an African American woman? His eyes bugged out, fixated on Mitzy when we walked into the room. He hadn't been ready for this development; it took him several seconds until he said:

"Welcome, welcome but I'm afraid we are not serving chicken or watermelon tonight." Nearly all of the people continued talking to one another but some laughed at him. That was the most appalling thing because it wasn't funny; it was an unoriginal, stupid cliche. Mitzy, having been prepared for Leo because I had been telling her for weeks about Rocky's racist, germophobic father, didn't miss a beat. She responded in this sugary southern accent that only a true southern belle from Yonkers could pull off.

"Oh, I am all right, honey. I had my fill of chicken, watermelon and even some chitlins for lunch today. But thank you so much, sugar, for thinking of me." She then ran over to Leo and took his face firmly between her hands kissing him smack on the lips. It hadn't been necessary to hold his face to keep him from moving. He was too stunned to move and while most had ignored Leo's previous remarks, Mitzy's words and actions got the attention of the entire room.

Everyone stopped talking, only Frankie singing *Fly Me to the Moon* could be heard in the background. Then the film sped up with things happening so fast I had a renewed attack of dizziness. Angelina grabbed her father, dragging him out of the room; Fran yelled, "Get your plates, the buffet is ready," and turned up the music to create more noise, and people started talking. It all acted as a buffer, but it couldn't completely drown out the F-bombs coming from the bathroom. It was a little awkward but at least we knew Leo had recovered from his shock.

♪ ♫ ♩ ♪ ♫ ♩ ♪ ♫ ♩

"Going to the chapel, and we're gonna get married . . ."

No chapel, it was the Oceanview Manor and Banquet Room in the Highlands, but my mother did pull it all off. The room was beautifully decorated with flowers at each table with a little gift bag and small bottle of champagne at each place setting. The only things she hadn't arranged were the photographer, the cake and a band. Rocky got the name of a photographer from Vincent and Sue they used for their wedding. We had already spent an hour with him posing in unnatural positions trying to look natural.

There was a huge table with Leo's wedding cake and assorted cookies and pastries next to the bridal table. I deliberated all morning about whether or not Leo would hold any grudges after the rehearsal buffet fiasco, but apparently not. I was prepared for the worst though, and I had already asked Ralphie if he would go to the supermarket if the cake wasn't there. Fortunately, that wasn't necessary, and the band I hired had also arrived and was playing canned music while they were setting up.

With so little time it was a no brainer for me to ask Gary if he'd play at my wedding. I naturally wanted to throw him some work too, since I was foolishly thinking I'd be singing with him when the summer season began again. Part of my thinking was the naivete of a first pregnancy, but I was also blind sided by him. I never thought he was eager to replace me. He didn't even know about the baby, only that I was getting married—my marrying was his excuse to hire Carol. I didn't even know I had been bumped until he introduced us. I had expected him to say, "Carol, this is Liz, who you are filling in for," instead he chose to fire me on the spot. "Carol, this is Liz, she used to have your job." In case that wasn't direct enough he continued in coded language making it very clear I was history. He kept stressing how "versatile" Carol was as a singer. It made me question why this was unsuspected as well, because there had been clues all along while I was singing for him in the band that he was not my biggest fan; he did love Carol though.

"Carol is a very versatile singer, when she sings *Material Girl*, she sounds just like Madonna and when she sings *Girls Just Want to Have Fun* she sounds just like Cyndi Lauper. It's amazing." I hoped they were not planning on doing those two songs, but I was confident Carol would sound like any artist she covered because as Gary said—she was, "a very versatile singer."

Someone chronicling my wedding day would say the worst was yet to come, but losing my singing job in this stinky little band was the worst for me. I couldn't even block out the pain with booze because I couldn't drink. So when Ralphie, our best man, who could drink, and had been drinking for hours, made a toast to Rocky and me and to our unborn child—I wasn't that upset. I felt sorry for my mother who had wasted her efforts trying to make this appear as a normal wedding. I also felt foolish wearing an empire style wedding dress trying to hide the obvious, in spite of the fact I looked good in it. Truly, those were the only things that upset me about Raphie's toast. Surprisingly, I didn't care how some people now knew what they had suspected all along. Yes, the bride was pregnant.

Rocky, who also got blasted, didn't remember Ralphie's toast the next day nor the fact that I danced all evening with Mitzy. Unfortunately, there are no pictures of Mitzy and I slow dancing to *The Look of Love* because the photographer left after taking pictures of the cake being cut. Kudos deservedly go to Gary and Carol though for sounding just like Sergio Mendes and Brasil 66.

♪ ♫ ♩ ♪ ♫ ♩ ♪ ♫ ♩

We were leaving for Miami Beach and Key West for a short honeymoon. Rocky had a bad hangover and I had my usual dizziness; riding in the limo to the airport felt more like a medical transport than the first leg towards a fun filled honeymoon.

We arrived safely at our hotel where we had booked the honeymoon suite in Miami Beach. It was all pink and white and I felt like we walked into a Valentine's Day card or the bedroom of a very spoiled, rich eight year old girl. There was even a heart shaped bathtub; did men really like this?

The very first thing that Rocky wanted to do even before unpacking was to lie down "to rest a bit." Three hours later he was still up in the room while I was down by the pool drinking virgin pina coladas and eating complimentary peanuts. Rocky finally came down to the pool but he didn't feel like eating anything. He ordered a bloody Mary, "to get my vegetable and fruit requirements for the day." I only looked at him; I didn't even smile. I usually laugh at his comments like this but I was losing my tolerance.

"What's wrong with you, Liz?" I told him I was tired so we decided to hang out at the pool, listening to the band and ordering tapas. We went up to our room around 11 pm and Rocky fell asleep immediately, while I searched for a movie. I was glad they had a television in the bridal suite; maybe we weren't as atypical as I felt. 1 hadn't imagined nonstop love making, we were not virgins who had been saving ourselves for our wedding night, but I did imagine we would make love at least once that night. Although technically this was our second night being married and that's when it hit me— we hadn't even consummated our marriage yet.

We were planning to check out in the morning, and drive our rental red Mustang convertible to Key West; yet I was determined not to leave that room until we consummated our marriage. I don't regret making the overture to him but he made me feel like I had been serviced. I got more passion from Patty who gives me foot massages and pedicures. I was not going to initiate sex on this honeymoon again; I'd book a spa appointment instead.

Riding in a convertible with the top down always looks romantic and sexy in the movies. When it is high noon and the sun is beating down on your head giving you a headache one is reminded—real life is not the movies. Rocky, shirtless, refused to put the top up because he wanted to get a tan. His obstinacy only irritated me more because he has a skin type that only gets redder even after hours in the sun. And when I tried to put suntan lotion on his shoulders he swatted my hands away like I was a pesky mosquito. I spent the rest of the drive holding a hat on my head with two hands to keep it from flying off—Rocky never got tan.

Our bed-and-breakfast in Key West was small but charming. It had a balcony where you could sit overlooking a garden with a statue of Diana. It was one of those quaint places that looked clean but had a hint of dirt and mystery; if you did find a roach in the bathroom you wouldn't be shocked. Even though I held my breath when I turned the light on, I liked it better than the honeymoon suite in Miami Beach.

The next day we explored Key West. I asked someone to take our picture in front of the US 1 End sign. Rocky didn't know why I was making such a big deal about it. I grew up in a part of New Jersey where we used US Route 1 everyday, it was a curiosity to see where it ended in Florida. Rocky was a good sport though and we are both beaming with smiles in that picture.

I did have fun on my honeymoon when I forgot it was supposed to be a honeymoon. We visited all the tourist attractions, the butterfly conservatory, Hemingway's house and watched street performers. There was a man whose thirteen cats were walking up ladders, pushing balls across the pavement, and performing other tricks; it was amazing, I never knew you could train a cat like a dog. I told Rocky I'd like to get a cat but he said, "No way, I don't want cat hair all around my house." Mind boggling coming from the mouth of a chain smoker. Personally, I'd rather deal with cat fur than cigarette smoke, but there were more serious things to draw a line in the sand over.

After dinner we decided to go club hopping. We didn't know the area, being typical tourists, and all the clubs we went to that night were gay. In the first club there were female impersonators; there were two Chers which brought some unwanted attention my way too, and Rocky kept telling me to get up and perform. Thankfully, it wasn't an audience participation night. I wouldn't want to compete with these drag queens, some were so beautiful I felt plain-looking in comparison: I kept checking my lipstick and hair all the time like I suffered from a nervous tic. Rocky and I enjoyed the show, and he wasn't even drunk when he ran up to the stage and put money in a performer's g string. I wished his homophobic father could have seen him.

By the time we got to the last club Rocky was very drunk and more than willing to dance with me. There was a huge dance floor on a lower level which reminded me of a boxing ring. Patrons on the floor above could look down at the dancers below like they were looking into an arena. Rocky and I were dancing in the middle of the floor, grinding and kissing. Since he was drunk I suppose one might say I was taking advantage of him. The patrons looking down at us started hooting and clapping and I still don't know why. Was it because we were the only heterosexual couple in the club or that we were so sexually uninhibited? Little did they know that the sexual energy was only a facade enabled by his booze and my wishful thinking.

When we left the club Rocky was staggering and could hardly stand. It was times like this when I sometimes asked myself—is he pretending to be drunk?—he was too stereotypical. If he were an actor playing a drunk person people would say, "He doesn't look real, he is too exaggerated."

We were a short walking distance from our bed-and-breakfast but there was a lot of drama packed into that ten minute walk. We had only walked a couple of feet when Rocky stopped to pee on some flowers in front of a shop. The shop was closed because it was 2 am but I was looking all around hoping no one saw him. That's all we needed, for him to get arrested for indecent exposure, or whatever the charge might be for pulling out your wanker and peeing on a flower arrangement. After he watered the flowers we continued to walk down the road, and he began to take his clothes off. I stopped to pick up his shirt so I was a little behind him when I saw two guys run out of an alley and head right for Rocky. They started taunting him and even though I couldn't hear what they were saying it really looked like they were about to jump him. What could I do? It wasn't like I could be Rocky's body guard and protect him from these two thugs. Just when I was considering our options they turned around, saw me, and ran off. Apparently, I had a more threatening look than I thought or maybe they mistook me for one of the Cher drag queens. It didn't matter why they took off though I was very grateful.

The next day Rocky didn't remember peeing on the flowers or taking off his shirt. Unlike him, I remember everything. If I were to pick a music track for my honeymoon, I would pick *I Will Survive* by Gloria Gaynor. One of the drag queens had lip-synched that song at the club we were at, and while it does not seem an appropriate song for a honeymoon, I think it is a perfect fit for mine.

2014

Fran had been living with us two years when it became clear she was having serious mental issues beyond forgetfulness due to only aging. One night she was wandering around the neighborhood in her nightgown, but thankfully was spotted and returned by a neighbor. While it wasn't as potentially dangerous, when she mistook the closet for the bathroom, it was more irritating—it was impossible to clean all the things that she peed on. Rocky was in denial at first, saying she must be sleepwalking—she didn't have dementia. Rather than debate what the cause was for her behavior, I chose to use my energy to convince him she needed to at least be taken to a doctor for evaluation.

In addition to those two very dramatic aberrations, for months now Fran no longer recognized me. She kept calling me "Aggie" and occasionally "Angelina" which was ironic because she didn't recognize Angelina anymore. I asked Rocky who Aggie was and he said she was Fran's older sister. He had never met her because she was killed in a house fire when Fran was ten years old. There would be many days where she was pretty lucid though even if she didn't know who I was, and she still drove her car to meet friends for lunch or shopping. I was surprised none of them ever mentioned to me that she was acting confused. Did she even know who they were or hadn't they noticed if she didn't? I only got a phone call one time asking me where she was because she was late for a lunch date. Maybe her friends didn't suspect there was something off with her—but she definitely was getting worse.

Angelina finally took her mother to the doctor's where she was diagnosed with Alzheimer's. I can't say I was surprised but Angelina and Rocky acted like it was a shock. Rocky even said they should get a second opinion. That never happened because Rocky went through the stage of denial rather quickly and became very proactive.

The first step was taking the car away from his mother which was not going to be easy. He told her he had to take it in to be serviced; she continued going shopping and out to lunch having me or her friends drive. Rocky gave her car to Angelina instead of selling it. It was practically brand new and according to him "cars depreciated so quickly it's better to keep it in the family instead of trying to find a buyer." I felt sorry for Fran because she kept asking me when the car was going to be ready. She wasn't forgetting that, and I questioned whether Rocky was premature taking the car away. That's until I found her one day in the garage on her hands and knees looking down at a grease spot on the floor.

"What are you doing, Ma?"

"I am looking to see if my car fell down this hole?"

It was frightening to think she had been driving on the road in this condition, and I did not question Rocky's decision to take her car away from her again. Weeks later Angelina came to the house in Fran's car. I was afraid Fran would recognize it, demanding its return. But looking out the window Fran only commented to me how a woman just pulled into the driveway who had a car like hers; no true recognition of her car or her daughter. Soon after Fran stopped asking me when she was getting her car back.

A few months after the car episode Fran had to have supervision around the clock, she couldn't be left by herself. I found an adult daycare center that provided care to seniors with physical or mental disabilities. She started going there three days a week and continued to see her friends on the other days; we also hired a caregiver who came to our house part-time. Fran was always with me, caregivers, friends or Angelina, but we still needed to change the locks on the doors to keep her from leaving the house by herself; the locks were analogous to making a house with toddlers baby-safe.

She eventually got progressively worse and went to the senior care center five days a week during the day; we also hired a home care worker full time who stayed through the night. We interviewed a number of people before we found someone we both liked; she was a very sweet woman from Nigeria named Tamarind, who looked like Sade—that was part of her appeal for me. I don't know if she could sing, but she did the job well—working six days and choosing her day off on the weekend. Fran liked her as well but had trouble with her name so Tamarind told her she could call her Tam. Surprisingly Fran remembered Tam—Angelina she never remembered—who picked her up on Tam's day off and kept her overnight. When she brought Fran home, she always said she didn't know why her mother had to have, " that live-in—Mother is a lamb." We knew she was keeping her drugged the whole time though because Fran was always hungover when she returned her. Fran has a prescribed mild tranquilizer that we rarely use, but Angelina uses it all the time.

Angelina causes more stress for herself and Fran because she's upset that her mother doesn't know who she is. Maybe I am not the one to judge, since my parents don't have Alzheimer's; I don't know how it feels to have a parent who doesn't know who I am. Fran seems very happy from my perspective though, and she enjoys spending time with Angelina, even if she doesn't know it's Angelina. They still have a relationship with each other, it's just different. I do try to look at it from Angelina's point of view. It is a primal need to have your parents recognize you; it is instinctive—your very survival might depend on it when you can't fend for yourself. Angelina is using the reptilian part of her brain. Now it's time to use your advanced cognitive skills, Angelina, your survival no longer depends on your mother calling you by your name. I never said that to her but I shared a story; I hoped she'd look at the situation in a new way. One day Fran called me three different names in the span of a very short conversation. I kept correcting her, I suppose I was getting tired of it. Maybe she sensed it, which considering her circumstances was pretty remarkable, and she didn't get flustered herself. She was very calm when she said, "What difference does it make what your name is? I like you, whoever you are." I tried to stop correcting her after she said that to me, and I am sure Fran feels the same about Angelina. Instead of taking comfort from her mother's wisdom, Angelina still insists on getting upset by being called the wrong name until she upsets her mother as well. She should be happy her mother enjoys being with her and has a good quality of life in spite of her disease.

It's probably selfish of me to say it, but life is easier now due to the progression of her disease. Not only does Fran like me because she thinks I am Aggie most of the time, I have help in caring for her in general, thanks to Tamarind. I enjoy my time with her, especially sitting on the swing in the backyard. She likes to tell me about the men she is in love with from the care center—a glimpse of an adolescent Fran; the mother-in-law from hell is now gone. Fran is nice since she got sick, garden time with her is another meditative ritual for me.

I am not the only person who has a self-serving perspective in regard to Fran. It's annoying when I run into one of Fran's friends and they ask, "How is Fran doing?" in a sad voice with pity in their eyes. When I say she is doing really well, they act like I am delusional.

"How can she be doing well if she has Alzheimer's?" I want to reply, "Why did you even ask me if you already had your answer." I'm sorry I spoiled their chance to show how empathic they were, but Fran was doing just fine, thank you.

2003

When I told my mother I was having twins I think she regretted having been so enthusiastic about the hand of providence. The hand was crushing me now instead of settling me and my mother didn't even try to hide her dismay when I told her. She wasn't negative about two babies instead of one, it was more a lack of confidence in Rocky. Since our wedding when he got drunk, my parents were not very enthusiastic about him or his ability to take care of a family. Perhaps my mother imagined that Rocky would react poorly to the news, but I had no idea what his reaction would be when I told him. My parents were wrong to prejudge him based on him getting drunk at his wedding however. I saw no indication, when away from parties or weekend bar hopping, that he couldn't control his drinking. He never got drunk during the work week and was highly respected at work, up for promotions in fact.

It wasn't very surprising he was okay with the news. I wouldn't describe him as overjoyed but his reaction was better than my mother's had been; his long range plans for me were a surprise, as well as disturbing.

"Well, our family is complete now so you can get your tubes tied."

I don't want more than two children but isn't that a decision to be made by both people in a marriage? Why was it his decision alone to make? Why was I getting my tubes tied? It would be easier for him to get a vasectomy. I told him that too, it didn't go over well at all. I finally agreed since he felt so strongly about it—I'd get my tubes tied. It was easier to lie than continue the conversation.

My having twins was not the only thing distressing my mother. She and my father were both very upset about our living arrangements. When we returned from our honeymoon, I continued to live in my rented room, and Rocky in his townhouse. Theoretically, it bothered me as well, but pragmatically—I preferred it. My rented room was closer to my job at vo-tech; the plan was to move out in the middle of June when school ended.

To be honest, there was more to it as well: within my own four walls the space belonged to me. *God Bless the Child That has His Own* was currently my song of choice. Rocky and I would meet during the week, and I stayed at his townhouse on the weekends—the same routine we had when we were dating. I continued to want to see him, but I would be lying if I said I didn't prefer to live at my place; I lied to my mother and Mitzy. To the former because she wanted me to have a traditional marriage and to the latter to avoid opening up the discussion again—did I really want to be married to Rocky? Mitzy never stopped asking, "What do you want, Liz?"

When I was dating Rocky the proximity of all his things was a connection I desired. Now that we were married, I felt like a guest in his townhouse: surrounded by his clothes, his furniture and his pictures on his walls. There was nothing we shared. There weren't even any shared memories of having chosen a single item together in his townhouse. No discussions made about where to hang a picture or place a chair. The idea that I might change the furniture around one day was as absurd as someone doing that in a house where they had been invited to dinner. My only belongings were some sundries in the half bathroom and clothes in a spare closet.

I told my mother and Mitzy it was a temporary arrangement; I did hope once we were in a place we had chosen together, I would no longer feel like a guest. Rocky's lease on his townhouse was up at the end of August. His plan was to be in a house before that so every weekend we were house hunting. You would think that would appease everyone but it didn't. I could understand why, it was already April. Rocky assured me there was no time problem when you had the cash.

We looked at houses along the Jersey Shore; not beach front property, but more expensive than other neighborhoods or towns farther away from the ocean. Rocky wanted to be near his parents.

"They're getting up in age, I want to be near them to help out."

At least he wasn't suggesting we move in with them; I shouldn't complain, nor did I have any power to do so if I chose to.

I had no say when we were house hunting. I didn't have any substantial money of my own to add to a down payment to yield any power. Rocky did ask my opinions about the different houses, but his opinions always determined the final decisions. The realtor was more attentive to my reactions than Rocky, thinking perhaps that my opinions mattered.

But this was an atypical marriage and I was an atypical wife. Most of the time I felt like a pregnant girlfriend.

We found a house in Belmar on River Avenue. It was beautiful—but way too big; we didn't need five bedrooms. True, I was having twins but there were still two bedrooms left. The entire house was more than we needed: with a formal dining room, living room, and a large kitchen—big enough to have a table making the dining room unnecessary. There was also a full pantry, finished basement and a little room the current occupants were using as an office. I've been living in rented rooms for ten years; any house would look big to me. Still, this house, as lovely as it was, seemed to be an extravagant expense and more than we needed. Disregarding my objections, Rocky made a bid. Every time I questioned his decision he said, "You like it, right?"

Of course I liked it. The best feature was the light all through the house. No matter what time it was there were windows that caught the changing light. The cream colored walls and lightly stained wooden floors added to the overall feeling of luminescence. In daylight hours you could always find the sun in at least one room of this house, no matter what time of day. It didn't need to be a sunny day either— when we first saw the house it was cloudy—yet it remained bright in spite of the overcast. If Rocky thought we could afford it, why would I object? The better question was—who was I to object? He wouldn't have listened to me anyway.

Rocky and I continued with our nontraditional living arrangement, but we had a closing date for the house on July 15th. I wondered how much we both would need to alter our lifestyles after we moved in together, since we were living like single people dating—not married people expecting twins.

I called him one night at his townhouse and a woman answered. I hung up checking my phone to see if I had called the wrong number by mistake—I didn't. I called again and Rocky picked up.

"Who was that woman?"

"Oh, it was you. Hanging up is rather childish, isn't it, Liz?"

"Well, who is she?" He told me she was a friend of Ralphie's. He was having a few friends over, and he did not appreciate me checking up on him. I wasn't doing that, but now he made me wonder: why didn't I hear other voices in the background if there were more people than this woman? Regardless, I was a wife simply calling her husband to talk, how was that "checking up on him"? You would think he'd be eager to put my mind at ease, to explain why a woman was answering his phone at 10 pm on a Tuesday night, instead of chastising me for hanging up. So why did I feel guilty? I told him it had been a reflex hanging up because I thought it was the wrong number.

"It's rude to hang up on wrong numbers." I couldn't disagree with him there and now I had lost my desire to talk to him. Besides, he was entertaining—I wished him a "good night."

♪ ♫ ♩ ♪ ♫ ♩ ♪ ♫ ♩

It was the final two weeks of teaching at vo-tech. I was playing a game when I told Rocky I might as well stay the whole month of June in my room since it was paid through the end of the month; I wanted to see what he would say. He said it was "stupid."

"What if you went into premature labor?" I told him I could have gone into premature labor before. He then dismissed any good feelings I had for him at the moment when he told me, "Do whatever you want, it's your life." Wasn't it our life, and the life of his children too? Maybe he was playing a game now, to see what I would say?

I moved into his townhouse when school finished, but sometimes crashed in my room the last two weeks of June if I was doing things in the area. My obstetrician was closer to Manasquan than to Rocky's townhouse: I would go to my room, lie down for a while and listen to music on my boombox. Most of my things were still in the room; I gradually took things out to my car each time I went to Manasquan. Mrs. Murphy wouldn't let Rocky in my room to take it all out in one shot because no guests were allowed in my room. I told her he was my husband, I don't think she believed me. Why would she? Would I be renting a room from her if I was married? She had a point and my parents agreed with her.

♪ ♫ ♩ ♪ ♫ ♩ ♪ ♫ ♩

For Mother's Day my parents sent me a card: "Happy Mother's Day for the Mother to Be"; it was really cute with a mama duck and two ducklings. Rocky wanted to know why my parents were sending me a Mother's Day card. "Shouldn't you be sending a card to your mother?" I did send a gift and card to my mother but it was a tradition in our family to acknowledge all mothers on that day; I told him my father always gave my mother a gift. Rocky told me not to expect one from him, "You're not my mother. You get presents from your children." Translation: I won't be getting acknowledgement in my immediate family until my kids start school and make macaroni cards.

I didn't tell the administration about my pregnancy. I don't know if it is obvious, but maybe not, I've been wearing oversized oxford shirts with stretchy leggings and muumuu type dresses. I plan to come back in the fall but I haven't worked out all the logistics. I am due late August, and I don't know how I am going to feel, or who will watch the babies when I am working. I am considering giving up one of my sections, but the worst part is I am incapable of walking into the administrator's office to discuss it with her.

I keep saying to myself: I'll tell her tomorrow; and then I don't. It's now June and not only haven't I told her, I avoid the main office and the breakroom. I have been eating my lunch at my desk in the classroom; I am avoiding people but not sure why. I'm acting like a shamed unwed mother, but when one of my students asked me if I was pregnant I didn't lie. My hormones have now affected my mind, just when I finally am not dizzy or nauseous anymore. I can hardly wait to see what happens to me next; it's no wonder I can't get myself to the administrator's office. I still have two months to work out the logistics concerning work though and I decided the administration does not need to be told about my pregnancy—I will be back.

♪ ♫ ♩ ♪ ♫ ♩ ♪ ♫ ♩

We had the closing three days ago, and I am at the house waiting for the moving van with Rocky's furniture and the delivery truck with the furniture I bought for the babies' room. When I walk around the house it looks big and empty. After the van and delivery truck arrived and all the furniture was put in its place—it still looked big and empty.

I always thought Rocky's townhouse was large but now his furniture is dwarfed by this house. Maybe it would be different once all the boxes were emptied, but it's doubtful since the unpacked items will go in and on furniture; they do not require their own space. The dining room and three bedrooms are starkly barren, and Rocky's furniture has a look like checkers on a nearly empty board. The only rooms that look completely furnished are our bedroom, the nursery, and the office—the rest of the house is open space.

♪ ♫ ♩ ♪ ♫ ♩ ♪ ♫ ♩

I wanted to run the vo-tech issues by Rocky but was I kidding myself thinking I could have an adult discussion with him about my job? My point of view hadn't carried much weight choosing our house, but this was about my job. I had it before I married him, surely my wishes had to be seriously taken into consideration, right?

"I don't want you to go back there. Why do you need that job? You have babies to take care of now. If you really want to teach singing, do it right here in the house. It's not like you need to work anyway, my salary supports us."

I was angry, but shocked at myself as well; I never thought I would be fighting with someone to keep teaching at vo-tech. But all the threads that connected me to singing, even the weak ones like vo-tech, were slowly being cut. First it was George moving away, then Gary firing me from the band and now being told I shouldn't return to my teaching job. Of course he couldn't force me to quit if I didn't want to, but he could make it difficult to continue by not supporting me. It was a waste of energy arguing with him. I did make myself a promise, however: I was going to find a new singing teacher in NY as soon as the babies were born—Rocky was not going to stop me. I was still angry with him about vo-tech though; I barely spoke to him for days.

It was about two weeks after our argument when I finally contacted the school to tell them I would not be returning. I had kept putting it off in hopes Rocky would change his mind, it never happened. If anything—he seemed more entrenched in his position than before.

On the day that I called the school I went shopping to distract myself. When I returned to the house, I sensed something was different. I slowly walked into the hallway looking into the living room—against the wall across from the window overlooking the driveway was a parlor grand piano. There was a little vase with a single rose on top with a card resting against it. I picked it up and read it:

I hope this will make you feel better. You can teach right here.

Love,

Rocky

I was shocked, and I felt the anger at Rocky I had been holding onto dissolve. I had literally quit that very day so the timing couldn't have been more perfect. Rocky didn't know I had waited this long to contact the school, he must have ordered the piano right after he told me to quit. And I wasn't sure I wanted to teach private students, but I was touched—Rocky bought me a parlor grand piano. It was extravagant, I would have appreciated an upright just as much. I couldn't argue that it didn't look good in the living room though; it helped to fill up the space. When Rocky walked in the house from the backyard, I ran to him throwing my arms around him, saying I could practice playing and singing now; maybe I could get a job singing in a piano bar. Rocky laughed, "No way am I going to let you sing in a bar with a bunch of guys hitting on you."

♪ ♫ ♩ ♪ ♫ ♩ ♪ ♫ ♩

Mother was planning to come to help after the birth. She didn't mind sleeping on Rocky's couch, which opened out into a sleeper. Rocky said she'd probably be more comfortable in one of the bedrooms instead of sleeping in the living room. All the bedrooms were empty though, except ours and the nursery; we needed to go furniture shopping: buying a dresser, bed and nightstand. After placing the furniture in the bedroom and adding a chair from the office, it looked like a monk's cell. It softened a bit when I added pale fuchsia curtains and a matching comforter for the bed, but the house would never win any decorating awards—unless there was a competition for minimalism decor.

My mother arrived two days before I went into labor on September 1st, mine and the country's official Labor Day. One might think Rocky would be off from work but he wasn't; holidays remain work days for public service workers. Fortunately, I went into labor early in the morning; Rocky was home when my water broke. He drove us to the hospital with a police flasher on the dash, which was unnecessary; it was unlikely I would give birth in the car. It was an uneventful ride, but he did get me to the hospital quickly. Before anxiety or real pain kicked in, I was safely in the birthing room at the hospital.

The days of only having medical practitioners in these rooms is over. My mother was amazed because when she had me and my brother my father was not allowed in the birthing room. As soon as I was settled, I asked my mother to call Mitzy. We had already planned that she would be with me and she answered after the second ring. I wasn't surprised, she was on alert these days since I might go into labor any day. She said she'd get there as soon as she could, "but you know what mass transportation is like, and I don't know if they're following a holiday schedule today." I told her to get here as fast as she could—I was already bored.

A woman in labor does not usually complain of boredom, but I wasn't in real pain. I had some back discomfort and cramps, like a very bad period day; not what I had imagined childbirth was like. It was only the beginning though, and I could hear women screaming and cursing from other rooms; I supposed they were further along than I was. From time to time someone would check how dilated

I was and my vitals; I was beginning to regret coming to the hospital so early. My mother said it was not too early based on the nurse's calculations, and kept telling me to lie down. It hurt my back more to do that so I kept pacing the room, driving her to distraction. I could not get comfortable, was not interested in the television, which was showing a picture with no sound anyway, and lamented over not having brought a book. Not that I would have been able to read it easily, walking back and forth. I couldn't wait for Mitzy to come to have someone to talk to; the only thing my mother said to me was: "stop pacing and lie down"—while she sat there calmly knitting. I shouldn't complain, she would also ask if I needed something from time to time, and once she asked if I wanted a neck massage. I appreciated her efforts but I did want this to end. It was like a type of torture; on the surface appearing painless—like water dripping on your head. After hours though, it became hard to endure because it was so monotonous, dull and repetitious. When Mitzy finally arrived at 1 pm it helped, solely because it introduced a change. She had made a tape of music for me and played it on a mini cassette player. The first song was Buddy Guy doing *Five Long Years*. It sounded so good, I wondered why I hadn't thought of bringing music myself. The speaker on the player was not very loud but loud enough for my mother. The tape was filled with tracks of some of my favorite jazz and blues songs. Mother wasn't a fan; she said the music was enough to keep the babies from ever wanting to come into the world.

By late afternoon the big pains still hadn't started, only insistent discomfort, and I was tired of walking around the room. Where were the big pains? I was starting to worry something was wrong. My doctor assured me everything was progressing normally; her estimation was I would start to go into the final stages of labor in a few hours. She also told me I had amazing core strength. Maybe all those years of pilates and yoga paid off, even though I hadn't taken many classes in the past two years.

I gave birth at 6 pm for my first baby and fifteen minutes later for the second; a full day's work. I had two baby boys; each a little over five pounds, enough weight and healthy—they would be able to go home when I did. When they were handed to me with their fuzzy little blond heads, looking like baby chicks, I said, "They have blond hair and blue eyes like Rocky."

"All newborns have blue eyes, Liz. But it does look like you got two little Rockys just like you wanted."

Mitzy might be right about the eyes of newborns, but I wasn't sure she was right about me wanting this. I never wanted to get pregnant, but if I was going to be a mother and have children with Rocky—yes, I did want them to look like him. Nevertheless, it was a little too late to have a discussion now about what I did or did not want in regard to pregnancy or motherhood.

Rocky showed up shortly after their births with flowers, a stuffed toy and a box of cigars. He dropped the toy on my bed and gave the cigars to my mother for my father.

"I had to get the cigars since it is a tradition, and I know your husband likes to smoke them."

I was sure those cigars would never reach Florida but it was a nice thought. I guessed the flowers were for me but Rocky just placed them on the table; it was Mitzy who put the flowers in water.

I asked him if he had seen the babies, he said yes, and that one was screaming his head off. "He's yours." I laughed, filled with happiness: Rocky was smiling, the labor was over, and I had two beautiful babies. Nonetheless, I couldn't get it out of my head that if I were to pick a song for this day, it would be Peggy Lee singing *Is That All There Is?*

Rocky and I decided we would each pick a name for one of the boys. I asked if he wanted to name one of them after himself. He said he always hated his first name but he liked his middle name which was Matthew; that's what we chose and we called him Mattie for short. I picked the name of Miles for my other son, named after Miles Davis. I didn't tell anyone but Mitzy why I picked it. When my parents and in-laws asked how I chose it, I said I wanted to have another "M" name. I'm glad nobody responded with, "Why not Michael?" It's good I didn't include the name-sake's middle name. I almost did—I would have had a hard time explaining where I got Dewey. Besides, Mattie was not given a middle name.

♪ ♫ ♩ ♪ ♫ ♩ ♪ ♫ ♩

Angelina and Fran dropped off food every day and my mother stayed with me for a week. She said she would have liked to stay longer but my father was lost without her. Mitzy took off from work for a few days after my mother flew back to Florida, and she also planned to come on the weekends for a while when my mother left. I was very grateful to them all—especially to my mother and Mitzy because I was scared to death of the babies. Not them, but how to care for them. I was more like an only child in experience since my brother was fifteen years my senior, and I never babysat for any child younger than eight. If the boys had been born talking, ready to play board games and toss a baseball, I would have been fine. I hadn't spent the last nine months reading books about baby care either. I suppose I could have started now but it seemed like there was never time even though I was being helped. The actual labor had not been hard, but after the babies were born, I was exhausted, and Mattie was always crying. It wouldn't have surprised me at all to discover that he was the one who Rocky said was "screaming his head off" in the hospital.

Mattie and Miles had very distinct personalities in spite of being identical twins and newborns. Mattie was hard to settle, he cried easily—while Miles rarely cried, and when he did as soon as you nursed or changed him would fall asleep quickly. My mother said Mattie was the smaller of the two and he probably got hungry sooner. Still it always took him longer to settle and was easily disturbed: if there was a loud noise from the street or someone dropped something in the house Mattie would wake up—Miles would sleep through it. My brother Ronnie told me about identical twin brothers who worked in a hardware store near his house; he referred to them as the good twin and the evil twin. They looked exactly the same, it was impossible to tell them apart until they waited on you. One was always pleasant, the other always disagreeable; if they were rude, sarcastic or impatient you knew you got the evil twin. I didn't think my precious baby was evil but I did wonder if their personality differences would remain after they were grown.

My mother and I got a routine going where as soon as Mattie cried for a feeding one of us would pick him up before he woke Miles, and I would sit in the rocker and nurse him. I preferred it this way, even though it took more time; I could bond with each child more fully. It was a philosophy I planned to adhere to past weaning. I didn't want to think of them as "twins," but as two distinct individuals. There would be no double vision dressing for my boys.

My reluctance to nurse them at the same time also increased after I saw a picture of a woman nursing her twins together. She was looking directly into the camera with a big smile. She wasn't even looking at her babies and it didn't communicate nurturing or bonding. Her face and demeanor looked like she was holding two prize watermelons on her chest. There was nothing Madonna-esque speaking to me from that photograph.

Our routine did change though after a few days when my milk dried up. My mother said maybe that's why Mattie was fussy, he hadn't been getting enough to eat. My doctor asked me if I was getting enough calories and drinking liquids. She also suggested nursing in different positions to encourage milk flow. She did say it could stop due to stress sometimes but there was no reason to think it would not come back. In the meantime I should give them formula.

Women in La Leche League would not appreciate my mother who said, "just keep them on formula, it's easier." That wasn't true, if one did want to feed them together it would be impossible—unless they had four hands; not to mention preparing formulas and cleaning bottles. I did agree with her, it was easier switching to formula instead of worrying about getting my milk back, or whether or not they were getting enough if it returned. Now our routine involved bottles and formula; the order of baby pick up remained the same.

After my mother left I continued to follow our feeding routine, it was only when my babies woke at the same time it changed. Mattie would wake crying as usual and Miles would also wake up but was quiet—that would not last for the entire time it took to feed Mattie though. I devised a new routine for when this happened: I would prop Miles's bottle on a toy next to his mouth where he could reach it on his own and I picked up Mattie, holding him in my arms to feed him. I was sure I was doing Miles irreparable psychological harm and was thankful they only occasionally woke up at the same time. Mitzy said I should get Rocky to help; I did try to wake him once but it was like he was in a coma, it wasn't worth the hassle trying to wake him. By the time he got up, I could have one baby fed. While that is probably an exaggeration, it still wasn't worth the irritation trying to wake him. I often thought he might be feigning sleep because he didn't want to get up. If it was true, I had to cut him a break—he worked full time; I was glad now that I didn't go back to vo-tech. Besides, I usually had everything under control; the days of being in fear of caring for my babies by myself were long gone.

I enjoyed synchronizing my schedule to the needs of my babies. For the next few months my days were a haze that had a meditative quality: caring for them, napping, reading, listening to music and singing at the piano. I would sing *Summertime* to them and Miles would fall asleep quickly. Mattie would look at me, surprisingly, not crying—he seemed to like music and my singing—I think the wrong kid was named after Miles.

2016

My mother always said enjoy your children while they are young because that time is gone in a flash. I did that and have many cherished memories of their younger years—it still went in a flash. I didn't overlook them when they were small; I am more guilty of that now, thinking that they are more self-sufficient. It's true, they are thirteen years old, yet when Mattie came in the kitchen looking distressed saying he needed to talk to me my first thoughts were: he failed math, or he didn't make the baseball team, or he lost his saxophone—or worse. I was guilty, much of my focus recently had been on what was going on with their grandmother. I hadn't been giving my sons the attention they needed and deserved. I had been out of touch, but I never expected what came out of Mattie's mouth.

"Mom, I think Dad is cheating. I saw him with a woman."

"What do you mean you saw him with a woman?" He told me he saw his father on the boardwalk eating an ice cream cone with some lady. My response was his dad knew a lot of people and was a very friendly person—that didn't mean he was doing anything wrong. I asked him what she looked like or if he recognized her. He said she had blonde hair and he didn't know her. I wanted to ask him a million more questions but I wasn't going to grill my son. I also wanted to play this down to put his mind at ease. It is hard enough at his age dealing with his own sexuality; he didn't need to concern himself about his father's.

"Why didn't you go up to him and say hello?"

"They didn't look like they wanted to be disturbed."

Mattie dropped a bomb on me when he told me what he saw. He would have no way of knowing of course that seeing his father eating ice cream with some woman bothered me more than the thought of finding Rocky in bed with someone. That was just sex—two people eating ice cream cones together, looking like they did not want to be disturbed, was a more intimate act than rolling in the sheets. I told Mattie to put it out of his mind that I was sure it was nothing; now I had to put it out of my mind. I could ask Rocky about it myself but I didn't have enough details, I couldn't lie saying I saw him; I didn't even know where or when. I did not want to implicate Mattie at all either, or ask my son any more questions.

There has been a pattern during my marriage when I suspected Rocky of cheating. Our own sexual activity would simultaneously plummet. Normally, we had sex four or five times a week. Sarah said that was amazing for people who have been married for as long as we have been. It always dropped to once a week during those times when I suspected infidelity though, and I had to initiate the sex. Rocky was always more than willing to have sex with me, and it was great for both of us in spite of my worries. Afterwards, I would ponder: had I been sending him subliminal messages, turning him off from sex initially? Maybe I had been acting aloof, even though I never confronted him directly with my suspicions. Perhaps, it wasn't his infidelity, it was my own imagination and insecurities that had created this sexual pattern of ours.

The only problem with that theory now was I hadn't been harboring any suspicions of Rocky cheating on me when Mattie told me his dad was eating an ice cream cone with some blonde woman on the boardwalk. But we hadn't had a lot of sex lately either. I thought Rocky was just tired, not that he was cheating. I had been planning to put on some sexy lingerie to seduce him. I once came to bed naked with honey smeared on my breasts, stomach and pubic area. Too bad I couldn't do that with ice cream—to send him a subliminal message.

2004

A year into my marriage I began to weave my web of deceit and lies. I didn't lie to see another man; I didn't want anyone but Rocky. I was deceitful and lying for my love of singing. I remembered this guy I met when I was singing with Gary's band who told me he moved into the area to be near the ocean. He said his wife would never have to be fearful of him cheating with another woman, but she was in competition with the ocean for his affections. Singing in front of an audience and getting paid for it—was my ocean. I was willing to deceive and lie to be able to do it.

It was a week before Mitzy and I were planning to fly to Florida with the babies for our annual trip to my parents when Gary called me. I hadn't spoken or seen him since my wedding so I was surprised to hear his voice. I was wondering if he was calling to ask if I could return to the band, but it was better. He knew a guy who had a restaurant with a bar in Trenton; the guy wanted to hire a singer who could accompany themself on the piano, and he thought of me. It was something new, one evening during the week when it wasn't busy; the hope being it might bring in more customers on a slow night. If I was interested he'd give me the contact information. Needless to say I was, and also glad

I hadn't gone off on Gary at my wedding for giving me the boot. The guy's name was Skip, and his restaurant was called the Alcove.

This is exactly what I was hoping for and wished that I wasn't leaving for Florida the following week. I called immediately—my luck was growing because Skip answered the phone and we set up a meeting for a few days after I returned from Florida. I told him I might have to bring my babies with me but I lied saying they were very quiet. I hoped the music would keep Mattie from screaming. I assured him if I got the job the kids would be at home; I wasn't sure how that was going to be arranged yet, but just that week I had decided to find a babysitter. Skip also told me he didn't want to start until the end of March; I wasn't worried, I had time to figure out how I was going to pull this off. We firmed up the time of the meet up, and he asked me to prepare something. He wanted to hear me sing and play. That was my focus. I'd worry about finding care for the kids while I worked—if I got the job.

♪ ♫ ♩ ♪ ♫ ♩ ♪ ♫ ♩

I couldn't wait to tell Mitzy about the Alcove, but not until we were alone on the plane. I was not telling Rocky. Not after his reaction when I said I'd like to sing in a piano bar the day he gave me the parlor grand. Rocky was picking Mitzy up at her apartment then driving us to JFK— definitely too much time to give Mitzy the opportunity to talk about the gig in front of him. I could wait to tell her when we were by ourselves; we had two hours and twenty minutes to talk on the plane before we arrived at Orlando Sanford. Keeping her quiet on the return trip was another problem, but I had time to convince her to keep my secret.

She told me I needed to "grow up." It is one thing for your parents to say that to you when you are young, but when your best friend says it when you're thirty—it really stings.

"You are an adult woman for heaven sakes, and he doesn't own you. Don't you have a say in your marriage?" She did make me question if it was my own behavior that always made Rocky react as he did, but he was the one who shot down my idea about singing in a piano bar; he had made his feelings very clear. It was true, I didn't stand up to him to express my own point of view, but Mitzy didn't understand, how could she? She was completely self-sufficient while I didn't have any power in my marriage. Our marriage was a hierarchy because Rocky made all the money that supported us. I loved my babies, but I was limited in my ability to earn money and power, by having had them. Not to mention the fact, the only thing I was trained for was singing, or teaching in untenured low-paying jobs. I wasn't Jaime, the doctor.

After Mitzy's reaction, the vibe between us was strained, especially when I asked her to please put it out of her mind. I hadn't gotten the job yet anyway, there was no point in causing a blow up between Rocky and me by mentioning it. She agreed, "but only because you didn't get the job yet, but don't blame me if you guys blow up, girl. It's you that can't be yourself with your own husband." That might be true, but what happened to best girl friends keeping secrets for one another?

For the entire visit I declined Mitzy's help with the babies. I would tell her to go ahead to the lake and I'd catch up. We had laughs and enjoyed outings together but there was a cloud that hung over us filled with my resentment and her disillusionment. I had to accept her help on the return trip. I found it too difficult traveling on the plane with two babies who were five and half months old without it. Maybe I did have to "grow up."

♪ ♫ ♩ ♪ ♫ ♩ ♪ ♫ ♩

Regardless of my conversation with Mitzy, I did not tell Rocky about the singing job. I preferred to keep my mind on my audition in three days. I went through all my music looking for something that was jazz but had a pop crossover; a song you would hear on a smooth jazz radio station. Some people say those songs aren't "real jazz" but they work for me. I finally picked *Don't Know Why* by Nora Jones. It had a jazz-pop sound and I had been singing it for the past two years: the right blend, familiar and easy to play—perfect.

Another preoccupation was over breaking down on the road or getting lost finding this place. Thankfully, it wasn't in the city of Trenton—I once had to pick my father up at the courthouse where he was defending a client and I got lost due to a detour. The Alcove was in West Trenton, an area I was very familiar with. I left early anyway in case I ran into any unexpected problems; there was no way I would miss this audition if I could help it.

Skip was nothing like I expected—I had envisioned an all American type because of his name—in reality he was a little Greek guy. He looked like Manny, the manager of a restaurant I worked at when I was in high school. And just like Manny, Skip had to look up when he was talking to me because I towered over him.

I put the babies in their stroller near the piano and gave each of them a pacifier. Mattie often spits them out and cries; I think he feels duped since no milk comes out. I had the time to park in a nearby convenience store parking lot near the Alcove to feed them before going to the audition. I hoped that would keep the pacifier in Mattie's mouth since he would not be hungry; so far things were smooth sailing. If my luck continued, I could get through this audition.

I sat at the piano playing a few notes to get the feel, and without thinking told Skip the piano was a little out of tune—I could not believe I blurted that out. It was like I was providing an excuse for why I wouldn't sing well. He didn't give any indication that that was what he thought. In fact, he seemed to be impressed by my knowledge so I relaxed, and I started to sing.

When I finished singing, Skip started clapping and Mattie started crying. Skip laughed and said, "Maybe he doesn't agree but I thought it was great. It's the kind of music I'd like to hear for my "Evening of Song." It sounded a little corny but I didn't care what he wanted to call his gig. I went over to Mattie, I had to hold him for the rest of the interview. Someone looking at that picture might think it looked strange, but Skip offered me the job. It was double the pay I had gotten from Gary in his band—for singing every Wednesday night from 7:30-11:30 pm. It was Skip's hope having live music would encourage the dinner crowd to stay after dessert to continue to drink, as well as draw in more bar patrons. The only thing that was daunting was Skip wanted me to take requests, in addition to the songs I had prepared for the night. It's not like I had catalogues of music stored in my head ready to easily access with my fingertips. If I were lucky there wouldn't be many requests. I left on a natural high, and Skip told me he would have the piano tuned by March 31st, my first night.

That night I told Rocky I wanted to find a new singing teacher in the city, and I needed to find a babysitter. He said he wasn't crazy about having someone in the house, you always had to worry about people robbing you. Did he mean kidnapping the babies? There wasn't a lot to steal; most of the rooms remained empty and there was no jewelry or cash laying around. Which reminded me—to finally mention the gun in the burlap bag laying on the floor in our bedroom. Our kids were only babies, but shouldn't the gun be locked up somewhere?

Mitzy's heart-to-heart had not influenced me to share the Alcove job with Rocky but it gave me courage not to yield to him about the babysitter.

"I hope you are not expecting me to never have any free time. Am I supposed to wait until the boys go to school before I can go to NY for singing lessons?"

He said I could always ask Angelina or his mother to watch the kids. But he knew I didn't want to leave the kids with Fran because of all the cigarette smoke. At least since the boys were born Rocky didn't smoke near them—Fran wasn't going to stop smoking because of the kids. Angelina had already refused to babysit for me; she apologized and assured me if it was only one she would—it was too much for her with two. She suggested that I put a notice up on the community bulletin board at Fran and Leo's church.

The church bulletin board seemed to move Rocky; he probably figured no one would answer my notice. He was firm though, if anyone did respond, they needed to be checked out; I had to get their driver's licenses so he could run a background check on them. Did he really think someone was going to drive a truck up to the house to steal his flat screen television? He said you would be surprised.

Soon after I put the notice up two women contacted me. I didn't even ask for the license with the first woman. She was very nice, it wasn't that I thought she would rob us or kidnap the boys, but when I offered her coffee she put ten teaspoons of sugar in her cup. I had visions of her giving Mattie a lollipop to shut him up. I wasn't an anti-sugar fanatic but I tried to avoid giving it to the boys. I would like them to at least have all their baby teeth without tooth decay, and keep them from developing a sugar craving for as long as possible. I thanked her and told her I would be in touch—I was interviewing other people but I would get back to her with my decision.

The second woman was named Kathy and she showed up with her four year old daughter. I asked her how she would be able to manage watching two babies with her daughter. She assured me it wouldn't be a problem because she had worked in a daycare center. She had experience watching more than one child at a time—where she had worked there had been a 1:6 ratio. If she was comfortable watching six I figured she could handle three. I then asked her if she would be able to babysit nights. Even if Rocky was home, he would freak out if left all night with his sons; funny how some men needed a "mother's helper" to watch their own kids. Since she had a young daughter she probably wouldn't be able to work nights, I would have to find someone else. It would cancel her out for my Alcove gig, but she could still work when I went to NY for my singing lessons. She said it wasn't a problem though working nights, her roommate was there to stay with her daughter. I didn't ask her about a husband, I didn't think it was any of my business. Rocky said later of course it was my business, I was interviewing her for a job. I did get her drivers license information—so he was appeased.

In the middle of March every year Rocky takes a golf trip with his trooper buddies to South Carolina. That's why he never wants to go with me in February to my parents in Florida, he doesn't want to take more time off work. Last year my mother was surprised he was going on a golfing trip two weeks before we were getting married. That's when she first started having reservations about him—way before he got drunk at the wedding.

Last year when he got back he was in a great mood. He was horny as hell too, and for the first time since he found out about the pregnancy and had proposed, he was as eager as I was to jump into bed. Truthfully, I was more relieved than eager, not that I didn't enjoy the sex. I was so torn at that time about the upcoming marriage, thinking he really did not want to marry me, that his eagerness was more reassuring than satisfying a sexual craving. A year later, only a couple of weeks before our first wedding anniversary, it wasn't the same when he returned from his golfing trip with his buddies.

Immediately, when he walked through the door I knew things were going to be different this time. He was surly when I asked him how the trip went, then he started whining about how all of his married buddies were cheating on their wives but he didn't—because of me. It was ludicrous, instead of patting himself on the back bragging to me how he had remained faithful he was complaining that he wasn't able to cheat like his buddies. He sounded like a little boy begging his mother for a toy because all of his friends had one. It also sounded like the grown up Rocky was asking me for permission to cheat. I gave it to him.

"Look, do whatever you want, okay? If you want to cheat, do it. I just don't want to hear about it unless you are wanting to end our marriage. And don't be sloppy either, cover up your tracks. Leave nothing for me to find or hear that makes me suspicious."

It was only a few weeks previously when he told me he had run into Jaime. At this unplanned meeting of theirs she told him that breaking up with him was the biggest mistake she had ever made in her life. I remember I wasn't angry or jealous when he said it to me. But I asked him, "Why are you telling me this?" He didn't answer me. I didn't pursue it. Infidelity wasn't my primary focus at the moment—preparing for my gig was.

I had found a singing teacher in NY who worked out of the Carnegie Studios. She wasn't a real fit for me because she worked mostly with people who wanted to sing on Broadway or in opera. She also was not working in the music business herself, she only taught singing, which made me miss George. Still, it was good to get feedback, and it was much easier to have someone play for you. When I was working on a new song I could concentrate fully on my singing. I would find someone who was a better fit later, but I was going to start singing in the Alcove in a few weeks. I needed help now—I didn't have time to keep looking for teachers. I went for weekly lessons working on new material while Kathy watched Miles and Mattie. It was only one day out of a week, nevertheless, I missed them every time I left for NY. But I was thrilled to be working on my singing again.

I told Rocky I signed up for a class at the New School in NY on Wednesday nights as a cover for when I worked at the Alcove. He gave me a hard time but I told him I was going to do it whether he liked it or not. I don't know why I couldn't simply tell him the truth about the gig with that same strength, but I didn't. He asked who was going to take care of the boys. Why he didn't automatically think it would be him was kind of funny, but I told him not to worry, Kathy was going to help him out. I know he was relieved but he was annoyed with me saying "to help him out." Not sure why exactly, since he himself had asked who was going to care for them in the first place.

By the time I started at the Alcove I had enough songs to fill many nights. I was still nervous about the requests until I finally assured myself I probably could work out the melody of some songs I didn't know the lyrics for; maybe I could simply play the piano without singing at times. Or if the audience was drinking and feeling good, maybe they wouldn't care if I made up words for a few songs.

I wasted energy worrying about it though because the patrons seemed to like me, although they seldom clapped. When I heard clapping it usually was Skip in the back of the room, but they didn't boo or throw anything either. Nevertheless, I discovered very early on that I was simply background music for most of these people—accompanying them while they were eating, drinking, and talking to each other at their tables. I definitely was not a singer they had come to hear perform—it was hard at times to keep my energy up. Even in the bars with Gary's band, where the audiences weren't always gracious to me, it was at least more exciting performing. Maybe if the patrons at the Alcove made song requests it would get my adrenaline flowing a bit more. Truthfully, I knew I should be chatting with them more too, mentioning that they could request a song; I should be making small talk about the songs in my program as well. That was a weakness, my inability to make small talk with the patrons. I was comfortable singing and playing but I was very self-conscious talking—the way some piano bar players were able to do so easily. I envied them for how they could sound so natural, and I hoped that my own ineptness in that area did not chip away from my overall performance. But were they even listening? It was hard to tell.

The last week of June when I finished for the evening, Skip came over to me while I was still seated at the piano. He said he decided to switch to karaoke for the summer starting the following week. He apologized for giving me only a week's notice, but he said he wanted to give me a hiatus pay as goodwill, assuring me that he wanted me to return in the fall. He added he could also arrange for a little salary if I wanted to do some private performances for him in the afternoon; he loved my singing so much. "Maybe we could even go out to lunch, right? My treat." That was a little strange, we were already in a restaurant. He then held my face between his little hands, forcing me to pucker my lips. I looked like a caught fish when he kissed me right on my restrained lips. Where had I seen this move before? Obviously, it was used when the kisser anticipated some resistance from the kissee. I got up as fast as possible, forcing him to release me from his clutch making him back up quickly, almost falling. I wouldn't have cared if he had fallen on his little bottom but that might have made an already awkward situation even more so. I was as disingenuous as I had to be to get out of there, so I thanked him for the lunch invitation with a big smile. I told him he did not have to give me any hiatus payments. I also explained to him how the day hours would not work because I was doing activities with my husband and children in the summer. I increased my volume by several decibels when I said "husband" so it sounded to me like I screamed it. I wanted to make the message very clear—to remind Skip that I was a married woman. I don't think it mattered to a man like him, but it mattered to me. It wasn't a lie about planned activities with Rocky in the summer either—we had tickets to see a matinee performance of *Wicked* in NY. I told Skip to definitely call me when he wanted me to return, and I gave him another big smile before I ran out.

There was no way I was going back to the Alcove. I can handle customers hitting on me, especially if the boss has my back. When it's the boss who is hitting my back—it is not manageable. It was perfect timing to end this gig anyway—it was just about the time one might expect a course to end at the New School. Rocky never suspected I was singing in a bar, he believed I was taking a music course in NYC.

I was now on an indefinite hiatus though. I planned to use the time to find a new singing teacher. I had already decided that a couple of weeks prior to stopping at the Alcove when my teacher, Pegeen, had her showcase. It was more like a recital for family and friends than a true showcase. There were no industry people there, and I don't think she had any contacts with industry people to invite them. Her showcase was not intended to help you find work; it was meant to be a venue where her students could practice their performing chops. I invited Mitzy but as usual of late she had a conflict; Rocky surprisingly was free and wanted to go. While I was thrilled he wanted to see me perform, I was a little nervous Pegeen might mention the Alcove to him. That's all I had been talking about with her since I started my lessons, and she had helped me with a number of songs that I had performed there. I would have to do my best to keep Rocky away from Pegeen before and after the performance.

Kathy watched the boys and we drove to the city because Rocky refused to take the train. When we got to the little black box theater Pegeen ushered me quickly into a tiny area off stage. We had hit a little traffic, there wasn't a long wait before the start of the show; less chance of Rocky speaking to Pegeen—that was fortunate. I had felt sorry for Rocky that he had to hear me vocalizing in the car all the way from exit 109 on the Garden State Parkway to the theater, but I'm glad I did because I missed the group warm up Pegeen led. My own vocalizing had been good enough and the show went off without any bumps. I sang *Stormy Weather*, the song Mitzy sang when I first met her at

George's showcase. After the show was over I was ready to get out of there as quickly as possible, but not Rocky.

"Don't you want to introduce me to your teacher?"

It wasn't like he was my dad for heaven's sake. My father never wanted to meet Miss Reilly in high school. If he had wanted to meet her, it would have been only to ask her why she did not choose *The Music Man* for the school musical. Nothing related to me. No, I really did not want to introduce him to my teacher. But I didn't say that.

"Do you really want to meet my teacher?" I laughed, hoping he would see the silliness of this; I was a grown woman after all—I only felt like a child with a guilty secret. He said yes, and I prayed Pegeen would not make any reference to the Alcove—my prayers were not answered. After the introduction was made she asked Rocky, "How did you like your wife? Terrific, wasn't she? She is the first professional piano bar singer I ever had as a student." She then flitted over to someone else, as lightly as one could flit when you were four nine, 190 pounds. When she was gone Rocky turned to me with this puzzled look on his face.

"Why did she say you were a 'professional piano bar singer'?"

"Oh, she must have confused me with another student. She has a lot of students you know. More than who you saw in the show."

My husband did not know the difference between a piano bar singer and a broadway singer even though I was the only singer who didn't belt out a song all evening. He told me he had never been to a Broadway musical in his life. Which I found amazing since he grew up so close to NY. That is why we were planning to see some musicals together. But tonight was not the time to educate him on differences between music genres; I grabbed his arm pulling him out of the theater before he became more inquisitive. It had taken a lot of effort to maintain my deception and I did not want him to find out about the Alcove now.

All the lies and deceit had all been worth it though—I was able to be a professional piano bar singer for three months.

♪ ♫ ♩ ♪ ♫ ♩ ♪ ♫ ♩

A good part of summer 2004 I looked for a new singing teacher. More accurately, I was looking for a coach, someone who could make arrangements for me as well as act as a mentor—I wasn't looking for singing lessons. There are a plethora of people available for the novice performer, but it is harder to find someone who works with experienced performers. I was not having any luck in my search, and it wasn't like I could ask Pegeen for a recommendation—that thought was what gave me the idea to call George. Why hadn't I thought of it before? He was thrilled to hear from me, and happy I was still singing. He did know someone, a composer/arranger friend of his who also accepted students to coach. George told me to mention I was his former student. Also, if I needed him to put a good word in for me he would. George said I would probably have to audition for him—that is how I met Stan.

Getting Stan to accept me as a student was easier than telling Pegeen I was leaving—which was very awkward.

Some people would be surprised that I simply didn't lie to her but I have never been comfortable lying; I was alarmed how easily I had been doing it of late. I did not want this to become a habit that crossed all areas of my life so I wasn't going to lie to Pegeen. I told her that I had learned many things from her, which was the truth—my breath control had improved tremendously. She was all about breath and posture which had served me well when I was singing seated at a piano. In addition to my praise, at my last lesson I gave her a thank you card and some flowers I bought in the train station. All of which was more about me trying to make myself feel better than thanking her, because I did also tell her it was time for me to move on. It turned out I was more upset about dropping her than she was about me leaving. She told me she thought it would be a good move, "I was at a little loss on how to work with you, dear." She then hugged me in her pillowy bosom forcing me to stretch my head up and back, and her face was smacking right in my neck. It felt like she was choking me; it definitely was a more awkward experience for me than for Pegeen. Maybe my apprehensions about finding a new babysitter were un-warranted as well.

I needed to find a new babysitter. Kathy was a nice per-son but she was a little too stupid for my comfort level. She told me she felt like a celebrity with private body guards because of all the nice police who came to check on her welfare when she was babysitting. Apparently, Rocky had his cop buddies coming over to the house every time she babysat for me. Did she really think they were checking on her welfare? Perhaps she was facetious, but why wasn't she also insulted? If I was working for someone who held such mistrust for me I wouldn't even want to work for them. That was one of the reasons, besides exercise, why I started taking the stroller up to the boardwalk with the boys. Maybe I could find some other mothers who knew of babysitters; get a recommendation from a person in the area—instead of putting another notice on a community board.

I didn't live far from the boardwalk; our house was midway between Main Street and Ocean Avenue. I didn't walk because the sidewalks were uneven; I preferred to take my car right up to the board to begin my stroll. Angelina told me I should go to Bradley Beach and walk with Fran, who walked on the board everyday with her pekingese dog in a stroller. Fran would not like me to join her, and I didn't want to walk with someone with a dog in a stroller. Besides, my main objective was to find mothers with babies to get babysitter information; I didn't need Fran's judgemental ears. I felt a little petty but I justified going to Belmar; there were several play areas on the beach there but only one that I was familiar with in Bradley Beach. I also liked the coffee at the Best Grind on Ocean Avenue in Belmar, located where a former chain coffee shop used to be right across the street from a playground.

The first mother I met was Beverly, who told me to call her "Bev." She was a little odd looking, she wasn't a fat woman but all her weight seemed to be in her breasts. It was pretty obvious because she was wearing a thin T shirt with no bra. Bev was definitely not very attractive and she made it worse by wearing these huge owl glasses and a silly looking safari type hat on her head. I only reflected on her being unattractive because her daughter was adorable. Genetics always amaze me—one often meets very unattractive parents who have beautiful children. Sometimes when the kids grow up their looks change but that doesn't always happen. Take Rocky and Angelina as another weird example of how genetics can be mind boggling—he is blond and handsome and she looks more like—Bev come to think of it. Maybe Bev's baby girl got her looks from her father, and hopefully they wouldn't change with age to favor Bev when she got older.

Bev was one of those women who viewed motherhood as a serious career and an art. She was very competitive and was always weighing her performance against other mothers. One of the very first things she asked me was, "Do you breastfeed?" That's when I realized why her breasts looked so big, they were engorged with milk. I hoped she wasn't going to whip them out when it was time to feed her daughter. I would have no problem with that if it was only us, but there were many people walking on this boardwalk. I told her that I breastfed for only a little while but then my milk dried up. She then started listing all the foods that would encourage my milk to return as well as drinking lots of buttermilk. She said I needed to stimulate the breasts too. Sometimes encouraging your baby to suckle, even though they would not be getting any milk, can trigger the flow of milk. She looked aghast when I said I was comfortable giving them formula and solid foods now. She told me she had breastfed her son who was in kindergarten until he was three years old. The image of a toddler standing up nursing at her breast was a real turn off. But I don't think she thought very highly of how I chose to feed my children either. I definitely got a very low rating in the breastfeeding category from her. It was unlikely I would meet her expectations in any other mothering skills and practices she was checking off.

I was just ready to start heading back to 2nd avenue, when another mother showed up with her adorable baby girl. This baby resembled the mother and would probably look like her when she grew up; the mother's name was Sarah and her baby was named Rosie, who was the same age as Miles and Mattie. Sarah was one of those people you meet and there is an instant connection like you have known them all your life. While Bev was one of those people no matter what the topic was you always have a difference of opinion— she did have a cute kid though. Looking at these two little baby girls made me wish I had had fraternal twins and one of them had been a girl. It was only a fleeting thought that disappeared as soon as I looked at my precious little blond-haired boys—I was glad I had them.

Sarah asked me what I did when I wasn't mothering; Bev hadn't been interested in anything about me other than my role as a mother. I told Sarah I was a singer. Bev told us her sister wanted to be a singer too but finally gave it up because she finally realized it was unrealistic. I often get a similar response from people in this area when I tell them I am a singer. They act like I am aspiring to be one—and they are not very interested—or they think I am bragging. I am not aspiring or bragging, so I get frustrated sometimes I can't talk about my life with people at the Jersey Shore. Sarah seemed genuinely interested though, and I told her all about my last singing job at the Alcove. She told me she was a high school math teacher but she was taking off for a couple of years to spend time with her daughter.

I decided it was time to ask them if they knew any good babysitters around here—that was the main purpose of my outing today. Bev said she didn't believe in babysitters—if her children were not welcome somewhere she wasn't going to go there. I definitely would never introduce this one to Rocky. I asked her if her husband helped out. She said of course and he felt the same way—no one should care for their children but them. I wondered why her son wasn't being homeschooled instead of going to kindergarten. I later learned she was planning to have him attend only kindergarten, after that she was homeschooling. I found her irritating, hopefully her son didn't. I admired how Sarah seemed to be able to completely ignore Bev, never reacting to her. She told me she knew a few good babysitters but they weren't around here because she lived in Jackson. She added that she wouldn't mind babysitting herself, if I didn't mind bringing the boys to her house. Bev made a "humph" sound under her breath. Sarah either ignored her or didn't hear, and said that we should exchange phone numbers.

I was eager to accept Sarah's offer right there on the spot, but I was not going to act impulsively. I would take the time to get to really know her—I was not ever going to ask to see her drivers license. I was hoping we could become friends. Besides, there was no urgent rush to replace Kathy; she was being monitored by the police when she babysat for me.

♪ ♫ ♩ ♪ ♫ ♩ ♪ ♫ ♩

For the rest of the summer I met Sarah on a regular basis. I was glad for her friendship, it seemed these days Mitzy was out whenever I called; if I did reach her she always had a conflict preventing us from getting together. I really missed her when I went to NY for my sessions with Stan; it was strange not to be meeting her after I was finished. When I was on my commute to the city, reading or going over my sheet music, then rushing to my class, I would forget about Mitzy. After I finished with Stan, I'd wonder why something felt off. Then I'd remember, I wasn't going to see her; for years I spent time with her whenever I went to NY. She was as much a part of the experience as the subway, the crowds, and the energy. NY wasn't as much fun without Mitzy, so while I often had time to shop, go to a museum, or walk over to the Central Park Zoo after finishing with Stan, I found myself usually wanting to head back home. During this period in my life my commuting time was actually longer than time spent in the city. I knew I'd feel different eventually because I truly loved NY—for now I preferred to go home.

By the end of the summer my kids were with Sarah at her condo in Jackson when I went to NY. If it was still early when I returned we would spend time together—having coffee or taking the kids for a walk in strollers. Her husband usually got home late because he had a long commute, and Rocky went to play handball at the gym after work. He went to the gym almost daily which was unnecessary—he had set up his own home gym in the finished basement of our house. He said it was different working out with other people which he preferred. It gave me more freedom as well so I didn't complain, and I never had to rush to get home on the days I went to NY.

Sarah and I also started meeting regularly two or three times a week, outside of her caring for the boys—we had become friends. For the first time I could really talk about my relationship with Rocky with someone. The problem with Mitzy was she was never objective, she had a long-standing bias against him. Before I could even open my mouth her response would always be, "What do you expect?" Besides her obvious lack of objectivity towards Rocky, Mitzy never had a husband or live-in boyfriend. She didn't understand how irritating it can be to live with someone everyday, sometimes you are annoyed hearing them chew. I could talk about my marital problems with Sarah and she could identify and relate. We also had the kids in common but they were not the only focus, or even the primary one in our relationship. Sarah was interested in other things besides child rearing. That focus remained with Bev, who we still saw at the playground in Belmar from time to time. I eventually also discovered Sarah apparently did hear everything Bev said; we spent a lot of time laughing about her behind her back.

While there was no limit set on Bev, I tried very hard not to be too negative about Rocky with Sarah. She hadn't even met him yet; I didn't want her to hate him before she even knew him. That is a danger when you use your girlfriend to vent all your frustrations and never talk about the good things too. There was a girl in my English class in high school who was dating a guy who went to a different school. She was always telling me how he called her fat, ugly, and how she would never have a boyfriend if it wasn't for him. I had no idea what she saw in this guy but I disliked him and I never met him. Who knows, maybe he had a bad day when he said those things to her, or maybe she said even worse things to him—nonetheless I really disliked her boyfriend. I definitely did not want Sarah to dislike Rocky. I loved him even if our relationship had its problems, and Sarah being a married woman certainly knew that all relationships have problems. Still, I made a concerted effort to keep a check on my venting.

I made sure to talk about good things too like going to shows and restaurants this past summer in NY. Rocky would hold my hand when we were waiting for our food, focusing on me the whole meal, asking my opinions about everything. He acted like a man pursuing a woman, not a husband with two kids out with his wife. It was very special and it was different; when there were other people around I often felt invisible. Sarah said it was because men were not as good at multitasking like women.

I also showed her the engagement ring he gave me for my birthday recently. Rocky never gave me one before we got married because it all happened so fast. He bought the ring at the same jeweler where he bought my band so they would match. I was very touched; I would have been even happier if he had gotten a matching band for himself as well but he refused to wear a ring. He said it was too dangerous to wear at work because it could get caught on something. It wasn't like he was a construction worker; what would it get caught on, or why not simply remove it while he was working? Sarah said that a lot of men didn't wear wedding bands. It was less of a tradition for men than it was for women.

Rocky didn't give me the ring on our first wedding anniversary. If he had, I would have thrown it at him—I was still angry with him on our anniversary about the cheating discussion after he returned from his golf vacation in March. I don't share cheating suspicions with Sarah. They are my dark secrets I now keep locked up. I used to share them with Mitzy but she already thought he was a player, it wasn't like I was providing a revelation for her. She never played the devil's advocate for him either; I was the one who rationalized for Rocky, because I felt guilty. Nobody forced him, but marrying me hadn't been his idea based solely on his desire. His days of playing the field had been abruptly interrupted, where he might have met the woman he truly wanted to marry, not one he felt obligated to because she got pregnant. I always carry this weight with me, and why I cut him a break sometimes when I think he is cheating. I used to share these dark thoughts with Mitzy, but I am not going to share them with Sarah. I had plenty of other things to talk about with my new friend.

It was nice also for our kids to have playdates with one another. Especially Sarah's daughter, who was an only child; it probably was a good thing for my boys too, to see someone new besides their sibling all the time. But who knows, I couldn't have a discussion with them about it since they were all one year old toddlers. They seemed happy, playing nicely with each other most of the time except for the usual toddler fights over toys. The only problem was when we took them to a diner occasionally—there was baby mayhem. Not between the kids, only Mattie's behavior alone. Miles and Rosie would be eating their food, behaving themselves while Mattie screamed his head off—trying to get out of his booster seat and throwing his food around. It was embarrassing, and since all the kids were blond like Sarah, I sometimes hoped the other patrons in the diner would think they all belonged to her. One time an older lady came over and I thought she was going to complain to us, but she was very sweet and momentarily distracted Mattie. She told us they were all beautiful children. Unfortunately, she also asked which children belonged to each of us—I had to admit to Mattie. She asked me what the age difference was between my boys because she didn't realize they were twins. That's because I dressed them in different outfits, not the same style with different colors but totally different outfits. I even styled their hair differently so she was surprised when I answered fifteen minutes. She had been very tolerant but Sarah and I decided to stop going to diners for a while. It wasn't a good time for us, the other patrons, or Mattie apparently.

♪ ♫ ♩ ♪ ♫ ♩ ♪ ♫ ♩

In October we had a spell of warm weather so I invited Sarah, her husband Joe and Rosie over for a little picnic. That was the only thing I could really pull off because we still did not have a dining room table or chairs. I had turned the dining room into a big playpen for the boys, closing it off with baby gates. But we did have lawn chairs, a picnic table and a wooden swing in our backyard. I also had a normal sized traditional fold up playpen which I set up in the backyard for the kids for the picnic. My mother asked me once why I didn't have a playpen.

"Why did you turn your dining room into a playpen, Lizzie, don't you have one?" She offered to buy one for us but I assured her that I had one already. I suppose a more interfering mother would have pursued the topic, but she only shrugged her shoulders with that disapproving look of hers she threw at me from time to time.

Sarah and I were a little nervous about the husbands meeting one another. What if they disliked each other? It wouldn't affect our friendship, but it might affect the babysitting arrangement—that's why I was nervous. I didn't know why it would bother Sarah, she usually seemed so laid back about everything all the time. Maybe it was simply that she wanted people to like her husband in general. She told me not to mind Joe if he didn't talk much; he was very quiet and it didn't mean that he didn't like you. I almost said don't mind Rocky if he talks too much; he is very talkative and it doesn't mean he does like you. I didn't say that, it was my private joke.

It turned out the guys got along well. Sarah was amazed. It was true that Joe didn't talk much and as usual Rocky was very gregarious. I suggested to Sarah, maybe they complemented one another—Rocky drawing Joe out and Joe calming Rocky down a bit. They also were both interested in golf, spending a lot of time talking about things that Sarah and I were either not knowledgeable about or had no interest in. She told me she had tried golf but didn't like it very much. I had never tried it myself but maybe if Rocky invited me to go with him I might give it a try. It was unlikely however that Rocky would ever ask me to join him.

When Sarah and I were alone in the kitchen she said she thought Rocky was cute and sexy. I knew she would know I was lying if I said the same thing about Joe so I just said thanks. I shared a story with her that Rocky told me which validated her "cute and sexy" comment. One night he pulled a woman over for speeding. She tried to get out of the ticket indirectly, trying to bribe him by exposing one of her breasts. I don't know if it really happened or not; he was always saying stuff to rattle me or make me jealous—especially since he had to add that he knew a couple of his buddies who would have taken the bribe. Sarah laughed, but she seemed to be a little uncomfortable by the story. It was surprising because nothing ever seemed to bother her, but I didn't pursue it because Rocky walked into the room.

Sarah and Joe stayed until it got dark but had to leave to get Rosie to bed. There was a funny dynamic going on as well. The quiet Joe kept talking, he seemed to be the one who wasn't anxious to leave while Sarah kept reminding him about their dog. Joe finally agreed with her that they had to get back to let her out. I had forgotten about their lab Sadie; she was always slobbering all over me so Sarah often confined her in the kitchen when I was at her house. Rocky refused to have any animals. He said when the boys got older he'd buy them a hamster. I'd let the boys take on that debate with him when they were older. It was one less thing for me to worry about anyway since most of its care would fall on me. I wasn't too fond of hamsters though—if anyone cared to hear my opinion about family pets.

After they left, Rocky said he really liked them and wouldn't mind seeing them again. I thought it might be possible to tell him about Sarah babysitting now. Surely, he wouldn't want to do a background search on them, would he? But who knew what Rocky would or wouldn't do. I was never sure what he was up to, or what he was capable of doing, so I couldn't be confident that he wouldn't ask me for Sarah's drivers license.

2005

George said he knew it made no monetary sense to fill in for a week when his vocalist took her vacation in July but maybe I could think of it as a working vacation. He would only be doing short rehearsals in the mornings so I would have most of my days free. My husband could come too; we could do activities during the day. George only knew about the husband; he did not know I had two kids to worry about, but in spite of the hurdles I would need to navigate, I said I'd do it. It was May—I had time to figure this out.

I intended to tell Rocky. I even fantasized he would like to go to Las Vegas with me. I was sure my mother would come up to stay with the boys; it was only for a week. Then I got scared. The problem with Rocky is there was never a discussion with him. He still functioned as a single guy, making up his mind about things without any compromise or consideration for me most of the time. What if he said no? Or didn't want my mother to come up? He'd probably leave the kids with Fran and Leo with all that cigarette smoke. Not to mention that Jaime would probably be visiting Fran as well. Fran told me Jaime recently separated from her anesthesiologist boyfriend. What an opportunity for Fran to orchestrate a family unit with her, my kids and Rocky while I was gone. What if Rocky told me—if I go, I could stay, don't come back. I knew my anxiety was making me think crazy unrealistic things because I was so insecure in my marriage.

The reality though was I was pretty sure that he would simply say, " No way." He could be so cold sometimes. He told me a woman he had broken up with had said that about him once and he acknowledged it was true. He never raised his voice, never appeared angry or got flustered, was usually completely in control—but as cold as steel. Unless someone had an altercation with him in a bar, and he had had a few—then he went off. Not his normal mode of behavior when sober.

Unfortunately, I discovered recently one could get frostbite from his behavior even when the temperature is warm. I bought a flowering cherry tree a couple of weeks ago because I saw them in people's yards the previous year and I wanted to plant one this spring. I didn't know Rocky felt the same way about petals outside on the grass as he did about cat hair in the house. I bought a small tree but it was still too heavy for me to budge. I had the nursery deliver it and put it at the side of the house. I was going to ask Rocky to plant it for me when he got home. I was excited because I had never even bought a houseplant before. I know it sounds silly, but I could hardly wait for him to return from running on the boardwalk to plant my tree.

The boys were napping and I was out in the yard by the tree when he ran up. As soon as he saw the tree he asked me where it came from and I told him I bought it. He said, "I don't want that tree. It's too messy dropping petals all over the lawn." I didn't even have time to say anything more before he lifted the tree by its skinny little trunk with one hand, and took it over to his SUV. My thoughts were also momentarily side tracked, amazed he could pick it up with one hand; after I recovered I felt awful. I hadn't even had a chance to tell him where I bought it, but the nursery name was on a plastic tag still attached to the tree. I hoped he was going to return it to the nursery; I didn't want him to just dump my little tree somewhere.

Rocky might have amazing self-control, but I couldn't control myself. I started tearing up as he pulled away with my tree. Then I looked up and saw Wally, our next door neighbor, looking at me. He didn't wave though, and when he saw me look at him he abruptly turned away. Neither I nor Rocky had raised our voices during our brief exchange. The houses are very close to each other on the side though—had Wally heard us? I was so embarrassed I hurried into the house, almost running.

No, there was no way I was telling Rocky about this gig. I was able to work at the Alcove last year without him finding out. This was definitely more challenging but I was determined to do it. The next day I went to a different nursery and bought the messiest house plant I could find. I put it in the spare bedroom where Rocky never went; I don't know what I was trying to prove, but it did make me feel better. I didn't feel good about Vegas though.

One day I had no qualms about deceiving Rocky, to only be torn up about it the next. I was deeply troubled over lying to him. It wasn't until I found the picture in the top right hand drawer of the office desk—then I no longer cared about lying. I was going to dust off my web to start spinning my lies and deceit once again.

I always go into that drawer for pens and paper clips. The picture hadn't been there a few days ago. There was Rocky with his arm around the back of some woman I had never seen before, both doing toothy grins for the camera. If I asked him who she was, he probably would say she was a friend of Ralphie's—that is what he always says. Women would often come up to Rocky entwining their arms around him, kissing his cheek and giggling in his ear when we were dating. It also happened once when we were at a karaoke bar after we were married. He never introduced me to any of them, and after they slithered away I'd ask, "Who was she?" He always said a friend of Ralphie's. Ralphie sure had a lot of women friends who also seemed to like Rocky.

I told Rocky I was going to visit my parents. He asked me why because I had visited them in February, and he thought I hated the heat in Florida in the summer. The gig was conveniently the week after my birthday, which is in July, so I told him they wanted to see me to have a little in-person celebration this year. Then I crossed my fingers, telling him of course he was invited, and he could come with me if he wanted to. I'm not a superstitious person but maybe when you cross your fingers it does work; he didn't want to come with me. I told him if he needed to reach me to call me on my cell, not the landline. My explanation for that was my parents never heard their landline ringing. All these lies, but my mother truly would have been the most angry hearing that one.

I wasn't finished lying though, because now I had to consider if my parents might call our landline. They didn't like cell phones, did not use cell phones, and preferred to call you on your landline if you had one. Lying to my parents was difficult but it wasn't actually a lie—more of an evasive machination which solved the phone issue. I told my mother "we" were driving cross country to Nevada and if she needed to reach "us" to call my cell, not Rocky's. She didn't ask why not Rocky's, only commented that a road trip that distance would be challenging with the boys.

"Aren't they a little young? But at least it's the two of you." Yes, she presumed Rocky was part of the "we" and "us," and I didn't correct her. I felt awful.

Sarah was concerned about me driving to Las Vegas with the boys by myself. She agreed to cover for me, but she made me promise to call her daily. She told me if she didn't hear from me each day she would contact Rocky. Not to rat me out—she didn't use "rat"; I don't remember how she worded it, but I got her message, she would contact him if she was worried about me.

It was going to take me more than two days to drive to Vegas because I planned on making frequent stops as well as staying overnight along the way. I had already made motel reservations with my auto club representative, who also helped me map out the route. My priorities were to travel on the fastest and safest route; I was advised to take Interstate 70 right across the country until Route 15 into Vegas. I was getting a rental car too; not as part of my ruse. It did help with the deception though, since I was leaving my car parked at our house—I was supposedly flying to Florida. There was no way I would take my own car of course—I was still driving the car my mother gave me when I graduated from college—it was ancient now. I was fearful of breaking down in the desert. A rental was an absolute necessity:

Sarah was going to pick me up to get a brand new rental, and I told Rocky she was driving me to the airport. Rocky usually drove me when I flew to my parents, so I picked a weekday to leave telling him he was lucky: he did not have to take off from work since Sarah would drive me. It was hard sometimes keeping track of all the lies.

Before I made my traveling plans I checked out babysitting services in Las Vegas—there were more than I had anticipated. Apparently, it was a popular vacation destination for families creating a need, since parents are not going to bring their kids when they go to the casinos. After talking to a few I made an appointment to meet up with a Miss Gilligan at Care and Love Sitters. I was ready and determined to do this; I had to pinch myself to see if I was dreaming.

♪ ♫ ♩ ♪ ♫ ♩ ♪ ♫ ♩

Driving by myself with the kids was not really that bad but I would never do it again. It wasn't easy; I was on high alert all the time. While I was driving I listened to music, usually Miles Davis, Diana Krall or Billie Holliday. When I wasn't listening to my CD's I sang. Sarah asked me how I kept the boys quiet when I drove all those hours. My secret was to keep them up to exhaustion in the motel rooms when we stopped for the night. I knew I would suffer once we returned to our normal routine back home, messing with their circadian rhythms. It was less harmful for them than inhaling second hand cigarette smoke for over a week. Besides, I loved having them with me.

The worst times for my anxiety were driving after dark or through isolated areas. I put a hat on the front seat passenger's neck rest after dark. It was a trick Rocky taught me to fool people to think I wasn't a woman driving alone. Anyone scoping out targets would also see baby seats in my car; we were an entire family to contend with—hopefully there would be easier marks than me— not wishing harm to anyone. I wasn't naive enough though to think I couldn't be harmed by someone during the day—I've seen those crime shows on television, but my greater fear was breaking down in isolated areas. I kept reminding myself: I always keep my gas tank topped and I am driving a brand new car—the chances of breaking down were low. Regardless, I was taking a chance; I wouldn't recommend it to other single moms nor would I ever do it again. When I felt especially anxious sometimes I would sing *I Whistle a Happy Tune* from The King and I. It worked better than deep breathing exercises from yoga and the boys loved the song.

I made it to Las Vegas with a fair amount of anxiety but no major trouble. I had more trouble finding our hotel and getting someone to help me with my suitcase. We were near Las Vegas Boulevard, walking distance from where I would be working. My first rehearsal with George was not until 10 am the next morning but I gave him a call to let him know I had arrived. Today, I was going to the Care and Love Sitters to meet Miss Gilligan to finalize arrangements for Miles and Mattie's care.

Care and Love Sitters had a daycare open from early morning until 6 pm, as well as sitters who would come to your place after day hours. Apparently, there were some very hardcore casino patrons in this city. I made arrangements to put the boys in daycare for morning care while I was rehearsing, then a sitter would come to my hotel room in the evening. I was feeling good, so far I loved everything about Las Vegas except for the heat.

When I was leaving the boys at daycare Mattie cried but Miss Gilligan told me to just go. She said children often acted out while their parents were there and Mattie would settle down when I left. I trusted her since this was my first experience using daycare; I crossed my fingers, taking a deep breath to calm myself, and walked out of the building. I was still nervous about leaving them, as well as going to my first rehearsal. I had been lucky so far, though, there was no reason for me to believe it would stop now—that's what I kept telling myself. I ignored the fact people say the same thing to themselves on a winning streak at the casinos too—and we all know how that usually ends. I simply refused to dwell on negative thoughts though.

I got to the club a little early; I was thrilled to see George. He introduced me to the three guys in the band: Julius on electric guitar, Tony on drums, and Rick, a double bass player. George would be playing the piano along with being the leader of the band. His friend who owned the club was not there, but he introduced me to the manager, John, who greeted me with a big smile.

"Cher, I heard you were in town. I am thrilled you're gonna sing at our club." Corny, but he did seem nice enough.

I was nervous before we started—I was afraid my voice was going to crack. It didn't, very soon it was a perfect fit—complementing the notes being played. This is where I was supposed to be and it was the only place in my life where I felt free to fully express my emotions.

It was empowering and my power expanded with every rehearsal and each performance—growing from the appreciation of the audiences each night and the acceptance from my band members. When I was rehearsing or performing I never thought about the Jersey Shore or Rocky. I still thought about my boys all the time though, especially when they were behind that door during evening performances.

I scheduled the babysitter to come an hour and a half earlier to the hotel before I had to leave the first night. I was planning to leave the room for a few minutes then return. I wanted to get the boys comfortable with the idea—when their mommy left she would return. I was dressed and ready to go to work when the babysitter knocked on the door. When I opened it I thought this woman was someone who had the wrong room—she couldn't be my babysitter.

Her name was Brandy and she looked like a hooker. Not a street walker, a very high priced call girl; she was very beautiful with long auburn hair and flawless pale skin. She had a terrific body as well—she could be a showgirl but she was not very tall. Whether a high priced call girl or too short showgirl, she was not how I had envisioned the babysitter.

She told me babysitting jobs were a side thing; she loved children but didn't think she'd ever have any. This part-time job gave her an opportunity to be around kids. I asked her what she did full time but she was very evasive.

"All kinds of things, but I have a flexible schedule. Sometimes I work days, and sometimes nights; it can change from day to day, I never know." I might have imagined it but I could have sworn she gave me a sly little smile after she said it—like she had shared a secret with me. I did not have to do a background check on this one, if I knew how to do that, she was obviously describing the work schedule of a call girl. There was no way I was leaving her with my children in the hotel room.

On my very first exit to wait outside my room, I called the club on my cell phone to speak with John. I asked him if it was possible to bring my kids to the club.

"They are very quiet and I have a babysitter. Is there a room where she can stay with them?" I don't know why I always lie about them being quiet. It's only a half-lie though, it's just Mattie who cries; my fear he won't be quiet encourages me to lie so often. My fear grew—there was a very long hesitation after I asked John if they could come, I was sure he was going to say no. It wouldn't matter if I lied or if they were quiet or not.

"I don't think the owner would like it very much, doll." Another long hesitation made me think he hung up.

"But if you're in a bind, okay for one night. They can stay in my office, but if they make any noise she has to take them out of there pronto."

I told Brandy there was going to be a change, she would watch them at the club. She said okay, not even asking why. My guess? In her trade she's used to going with the flow of other people. When we got to the club John took us to his office, which was directly across from stage right; I could see the office door from the stage. If I had bells to hang on the door I would also hear Brandy if she opened it trying to abscond with my kids—the band would have to be playing very softly. I wasn't serious, I was trying to make myself laugh, remembering Rocky who always says, "chimes prevent crimes." Truthfully, it did make me less anxious being able to see the office door from the stage though. I also could see almost immediately that John was enamored with Brandy. He spent a lot of time in his office that night and when we left he called out to us, "Am I going to see you tomorrow, doll?" I thought he was talking to me, but I realized it was Brandy when she replied, "Well, I am babysitting all week." John grunted his approval—I guess my kids making noise and the owner were no longer problems for him. I hated to break this blooming relationship up but I was getting a different babysitter.

The next morning when I dropped the kids off at daycare, I asked Miss Gilligan if there was someone other than Brandy who could watch the boys. She asked me if there was a problem: I said no but Brandy mentioned she occasionally worked some nights at another job; was there someone else available if she couldn't work? She told me Brandy had committed to the full week; she did not anticipate a problem, but she was the only person in her pool available. The only other woman who was free, she had asked before Brandy, refused to care for toddler twins.

Do people realize how difficult it is for a single woman with a kid? Some may, but they might not realize when it is more than one—it can be downright daunting. I can't even imagine what women do without help or if they don't have the financial means to manage comfortably. It is more difficult to find babysitters, and simply trying to do shopping or physically maneuvering with more than one is extremely challenging—if not impossible at times. That was one of the reasons why I chose to drive, because all the carriers I contacted required two adults to be on the plane with kids my age. I never fully appreciated the difficulty of having young children close in age until making this trip. I always thought it was awful when I saw a parent using a toddler leash and harness for their children as though they were dogs. I am now forgiving since I used them for this trip, and I wouldn't have been able to function at times without those innovative restraints. I didn't have much control in regard to babysitters in Vegas however.

I didn't have a choice. I contacted other agencies but they did not have anyone available to babysit; or like Care and Love Sitters, when sitters were available they did not want to watch twins. Had there been a notorious incident of knife wielding toddler twins attacking a babysitter in Vegas I was not aware of? Making myself laugh always took the edge off a bit but I was still stuck with Brandy.

I kept my eye on John's office door a lot throughout the performances, glad I could angle myself in such a way on the stage not to be too obvious to the audience. Brandy continued to babysit for me all week at the club, while John was in the office with her most of the time. I tried to concentrate on my songs and I did pretty well, but it was hard to keep myself from imagining what Brandy and John were doing behind that door.

2010

For the next five years my web did not collect any dust, which reminded me of something Leo said at one of the Sunday family meals. He was a notorious liar according to him—lied all the time because he didn't want people to know his business—with one disclaimer: "I only lie to people I don't like and never to close family. You gotta have someone you can tell the truth to." I agreed with him and I didn't lie to Sarah. She was the only one who knew what I was really doing; I did lie to my close family. After the first year, I was not just evasive with my parents—I shamefully lied full out. Ironically, I never lied to them when I was a teenager, now as a grown woman—I was doing it on a regular basis; I hadn't been a rebellious teenager. I read once that if a girl doesn't rebel in her teens, she will often rebel in her thirties. Is that what happened to me? I continued to deceive Rocky as well.

The narrative to Rocky was always the same—I was visiting my parents in July for two weeks. Sarah continued to cover for me, as well as to take me to get my rental car. Gradually, Rocky stopped asking if I wanted him to drive me to the airport since I always told him Sarah would do it.

I didn't drive to Las Vegas. I never did that again, but having done it, I didn't have any qualms about driving to my parents in Florida—which was half the distance. It was a well travelled route with a lot of rest stops and no isolated desert expanses. I had no fears of breaking down on a lonely highway. I always made one overnight stop in North Carolina as well; I didn't do any night driving on these trips. Marianne had gotten married since I last saw her at my wedding and had moved to North Carolina with her husband Barry. Her house was conveniently located about half the distance to my parents. The first time I drove to Florida, we stayed in a motel near her on the trip down, meeting them for dinner. On our return she insisted we stay with her, and invited me to stay with her for all my subsequent trips. They lived in a big Victorian house in Burlington Barry inherited from his grandmother. It was generous of them, even though I am one of those rare people who like motels as long as they are clean with no musty smells. I also don't mind the small space of a motel room. I had lived in rented rooms for ten years, but the boys loved running around in their big backyard. I took Marianne up on her offer, and her house became our stop over on the way to and from Florida for all those years.

I often planned activity stops for the boys along the way during those years too, and as they got older it was truly fun being on the road with them; we were able to really bond during that time. Still, it was easier after arriving in Florida to leave them with my parents when I flew to Vegas. Once they were safely with grandma and grandpa, I didn't have to worry about their welfare, or entertaining them, or hooker babysitters. I could focus totally on my singing.

I told my parents I needed to get away by myself each year; a kind of informal retreat. I asked them if they would mind watching the boys for me because Rocky could not watch the kids due to his work, and I still had an issue with Fran and Leo—who continued to puff away. Their dog even had trouble breathing from their cigarette smoke. She was one of those breeds with a pushed in nose and was quite old, so whenever I mentioned the dog's struggle to breathe to Rocky he focused only on her age, not the smoke. "That dog is ancient. I'm surprised it can do anything. They should put it out of its misery." The poor dog's wheezing might have been due to age, but second hand smoke can't be good for dogs any more than it is for humans—especially little humans. Nobody or anything could get Fran or Leo to stop smoking. Leo smoked up to his dying day; he didn't even stop when he was diagnosed with emphysema, which eventually killed him.

Second hand smoke exposure was not the only excuse I gave my parents for needing them; Mattie was a little intimidated by Leo and it started when he was a baby. Leo was a very animated storyteller; he could have been an actor since he seemed to live and breathe his tale in the telling. The only problem was his stories were usually about fights or altercations where he was battling an invisible foe— shouting loudly, sometimes forcefully pounding the table— scaring Mattie: Mattie would cry and Leo would feel bad.

"Oh, Mattie, did I scare you? I'm sorry, honey, I don't want to scare him. Come to Poppy." Mattie would refuse to go to him and continued to cry.

When Mattie got older Rocky would yell at him, "Stop crying and go to Poppy, you're making him feel bad," which only made it worse. The reality, regardless of Mattie's anxiety or my concern about second hand smoke, leaving the boys with Rocky's parents didn't fit my ruse as well as saying I was visiting my parents. And I didn't have to work very hard trying to convince my parents to watch the boys while I went to Vegas.

My parents loved seeing them twice in one year. Mattie and Miles were their only grandchildren, and probably would always be their only grandchildren. I didn't think Ronnie and Joann were ever going to have kids. When I visited my parents in February, the boys and I were with my brother and Joann. My parents could not completely focus on Miles and Mattie because there were too many people demanding their attention. They liked the July visit because they could spoil them rotten, and I wouldn't even be there to monitor the giving of sweets or toys. They usually took them to Disney World too which amazed me. I couldn't comprehend how my parents could stand in those lines in the hot summer sun. They told me the lines were shorter in the summer; I suppose they were also better acclimated to the heat compared to other people, golfing all year in Florida. I certainly did not inherit a tolerance to the heat from them.

Why had I never told them I was going to Las Vegas? It didn't sound like a retreat destination, and they might start to question why I was going there every year. I was too insecure to share the job with them; I feared somehow Rocky might find out and take it away from me. So I openly lied to them instead of telling them about my singing gig or Vegas.

Over that five year period I told them I was going to Maine twice, and for the other years to New Hampshire,

Massachusetts and Vermont. I favored New England because the climate would have been preferable. The only thing I hate about Vegas is the heat; it feels like someone is blowing a hair dryer in your face on high. I never understand why locals say, "Yes, it's hot. But it's a dry heat," like that makes it better. I prefer the Florida heat, at least it has some moisture in it. In Vegas my skin feels like dried out parchment paper.

The first year I left the boys with grandma and grandpa I told them I was going to Portland, Maine. My father asked me if I could bring back maple syrup. I wondered if there was a Canada casino in Vegas. I told him I probably couldn't bring syrup on the plane—with all the restrictions these days. Sometimes it did get complicated; too many strands on the web.

After he asked me that I hurried out of there, saying I was running late: I had to drive to Orlando Sanford to catch my plane. I had plenty of time, but I didn't want to give him time to remember those little maple candies he also liked. I could probably find some maple syrup made in Canada in some grocery store in Vegas, but I didn't think I could find those candies anywhere.

When I got to the club in Vegas, the first year the kids were with my folks, John asked me where they were. He looked a little disappointed when I told him they were with my parents—I knew his disappointment had nothing to do with my kids. George looked puzzled saying he didn't even know I had children. Maybe he never noticed them the year before, or if he had, did he think they belonged to Brandy? With her fair skin and blue eyes, she had looked more like their mother than me.

During all the years singing with the band, I was with the same guys I worked with the first year. For one full week each year I felt accomplished, and had a sense of self-worth—sorely missing in my life at the Jersey Shore. The audiences liked me too. Someone who was a local and a regular fan of the band even told me I was better than Denise, who I was filling in for. He might have been just flirting, but it did make me feel good.

Singing with the band filled me completely with joy. It was sweet, lasting nourishment. If I kept busy with my kids and worked with Stan on my vocals, in spite of returning to the Jersey Shore, it could often sustain me until I walked into the club the following year. Singing in Vegas was not without its negatives though. When I told my parents I was going to Portland, Maine, again in year four, my mother asked me to check if that cute little bakery was still by the ferry at Casco Bay. There was always something that would remind me of my deception, and it piled up over the years. In college we read Walter Scott's epic poem, *Marmion* in a world literature course. I did not enjoy it, but one line is memorable: "Oh what a tangled web we weave, when first we practice to deceive." He is right about that, very little has changed from the 19th century on that score.

♪ ♫ ♩ ♪ ♫ ♩ ♪ ♫ ♩

When the boys turned seven I dismantled the web, making a vow I would never lie again for the rest of my life. I found an overnight camp for them during the time I would be in Las Vegas singing. My parents were very disappointed when I told them they didn't have to care for the boys. I promised to stay a little longer in February to make up for it, but of course I would be there as well, hampering their spoiling a bit. Maybe sending the boys to camp when I went to Vegas, instead of to my parents', irritated my mother, making her ask, "Isn't that where you've been going all these years?" She surprised me, but I was serious about not lying anymore, so I told her—yes, asking for her forgiveness. I also tried to explain why I had lied—I wasn't trying to excuse my behavior; I only wanted to try to make her understand why I deceived her. Maybe then she might be able to clarify it for me. I asked her how she knew, and she said it didn't take a detective to figure it out. I hoped she wasn't trying to give me a veiled hint about Rocky. She also told me that I needed to develop some grit if I was going to stay in my marriage—or did I want to get out of it?

"How can you stay in a marriage where you can't pursue your desires?" I asked her how she was pursuing her desires running around all day long trying to meet every need of my father's ever since they moved to Florida. She answered me without a second's thought.

"What makes you think that's not what I desire?" I respected her feelings, and I love Rocky, but I wondered if that would ever be enough to fully satisfy me. Maybe if I was secure in feeling he loved me it would be, but this was all hypothetical. Sometimes I even question if it is possible to love someone when you have been deceiving them.

When I told Rocky I was going to Vegas when the boys were at camp to sing with George's band, he said he didn't want me to be singing in a bar with a lot of drunks. I guess he was familiar with drunks since he usually was one of them. I said he could come with me and I meant it. It would be fun, we hadn't had a vacation just the two of us since the honeymoon. I didn't think about the fact that my long running deception might be revealed when I asked him to join me. It was only later that that occurred to me, so I was glad he said he couldn't take time off. He still had a problem about guys hitting on me in a bar, though, but I assured him that George would be right there. He wouldn't let anyone mess with me, and George was not some fragile boned delicate soul like the homosexual stereotype. He was very macho, he could take someone apart using his two fists or his cutting tongue.

Rocky then said it was ridiculous pay, because after expenses I would only be left with a few dollars. I said at least I'd have some money after expenditures, unlike him when he took his annual golfing trip with his buddies. He still didn't budge.

My final argument was in the form of a compromise. It could be a win-win or lose-lose compromise—that depended on Rocky. I was giving him the power to decide, but I chose to present the lose-lose scenario first for his consideration. If he agreed to give up his golfing trip, I would give up my job. When I said "job" I tried to make it very clear through volume and stress that it had higher ranking than golf; although that probably hadn't swayed his thinking at all. The truth is he would never give up his yearly golfing trip with his buddies. And he finally backed off making me ask myself—if I had stood up to him years ago could I have avoided lies and deception? No, it was easy to be strong when the kids were not in the mix, and he couldn't use them as pawns to get me to do what he wanted.

My audacity surprised me more than him when I asked him to drive me to the airport in a week's time. "What's the matter, Sarah is no longer available?" I told him, truthfully, that I didn't know, but preferred that he take me and he grudgingly agreed. I had made a vow never to lie again but I also was not about to make a confession about the last seven years either—revealing that Sarah never drove me to the airport.

The ride to the airport the following week was painful though. Rocky was in his cold steel mode. For the entire drive the silence was like a shroud enveloping the car. This was a man who was called talkative at best and a blabber mouth at worst. Sometimes, when we watched a DVD I would have to pause and rewind it because he was talking too much; now he would only talk when answering my questions using monosyllabic responses. I kept trying to engage him in a conversation but it was impossible to cut through the fog that was keeping us apart. What did become clear to me that day—what I had always thought was a commendable ability for self-control, was really passive aggressiveness. So I simply stopped trying to get him to talk to me, preferring to go over my new songs in my head for the better part of the drive.

♪ ♫ ♩ ♪ ♫ ♩ ♪ ♫ ♩

Vegas continued to be rewarding, George even said he wished he could hire me full time. He was serious: if I ever wanted to move there to let him know. George's support and respect were always something that drew me back each year but it was only the frosting on the cake. The opportunity to sing was paramount, and being accepted as a fellow professional by the other band members was very important to me as well. What always surprised me too was I only worked with them for one week each year yet it felt like it was only yesterday when I returned. I was treated like an equal, and I felt like a different person for one week every year; a Cinderella at the ball in Vegas story in an annual replay.

How could I be so valued and respected in Vegas, yet be treated like a child, who was not allowed to make her own decisions about her life at the Jersey Shore? Of course at the Jersey Shore there wasn't only my life to consider; the lives of Rocky and the boys needed to be considered as well. Still, the lack of respect and equality were sore points when I returned after working in Vegas each year.

At the Jersey Shore there was a pecking order—I was not equal to Rocky, and who knew where I'd end up by the time Miles and Mattie got older. It's a fact some boys model their father's behavior when they're grown, to treat their mothers and wives the same way they saw their father behaving towards women. It's a tainted legacy and my being submissive to Rocky was not good modelling for them either. They should at least see that a woman might stand up to them.

♪ ♫ ♩ ♪ ♫ ♩ ♪ ♫ ♩

I had no desire to have Rocky pick me up at the airport on my return to take another long silent drive. I preferred making four train transfers, with a wheeled carrier to pull my suitcase, and a good novel to read on the trains. I was also still floating on a natural high note—I did not want Rocky to make me crash early. Crashes are inevitable after the high of performing, which has nothing to do with anyone—why induce it before it would occur naturally? He was surly when I told him I'd take the train home and he didn't have to take off from work to pick me up at the airport. Was his mood new, or simply a carry over from the previous week? It was hard to tell but it didn't matter—I got off my phone as soon as possible.

The surliness continued when I got home and it might have developed into something more threatening to our marriage, I'll never know for sure. Sadly, Leo died two days after my return, making Rocky vulnerable—and he needed me. I never wanted Rocky to feel bad in order to make me feel valued and wanted, but the only times I truly feel secure about where I fit into his life is when he is insecure himself.

There were two times when Rocky truly had meltdowns: after the horrific crash on the Garden State Parkway and when Leo died. It scared me the first time—seeing him break down crying, all his tough macho facade melting away to reveal the little boy who still lives there. And just like that first time, on the day Leo died, I again held him in my arms whispering that I loved him, repeating over and over that everything was going to be alright. I hope I will not be damned for feeling so powerful when I did it.

People who really didn't know Leo well wondered why the family was taken by surprise when he died, since he had had heart problems and emphysema for years. They didn't know him well: he had such a strong personality;

he was another force of nature. If anyone could live to a hundred in spite of their illnesses it would be him. I would not have been surprised if he had blown himself up—he refused to stop smoking near his oxygen tank—but his heart and lungs giving out were truly a surprise. The greatest legacy Leo left Rocky was the catalyst to give up smoking cold turkey. Rocky then cajoled his mother to quit too. She started smoking again but finally by the holidays she kicked the habit as well.

I would miss Leo. It's true, he could say some awful things and be really mean to some people. But if he liked you he could be very kind too, literally giving you the shirt off his back. Or to be more accurate, his coat. Fran liked to tell the story, when they were young still living in the South Bronx, how Leo came home from the family bakery one evening in the middle of winter without his coat. Fran asked, "What happened to your coat?" At first he wouldn't tell her. He finally admitted that in addition to sandwiches, he also gave his coat to the homeless man who slept near their bakery. I hoped someone would tell that story at his funeral.

I didn't want to bring the boys to the wake so Sarah was going to watch them. They weren't babies and they had a concept of death, but never had a direct experience with it—not even the death of a beloved pet since they never had one. I didn't want their first experience to be seeing their grandfather in a coffin. Joe dropped Sarah and Rosie off at our house while he went to the wake to support Rocky. Joe and Rocky had continued to be friends since they met at our picnic, frequently golfing together, which amazed Sarah because she still thought they were an odd couple.

I was glad Rocky didn't give me a hard time over the boys not going to the wake; wakes were even difficult for some adults. I had only been to one before, Kenny's grandmother's wake when I was in high school. I remember how weird it was hearing people say how good she looked. I wouldn't know because I never met her so I didn't know what she looked like alive—but how good can one look dead? Maybe they meant she looked peaceful, which makes us feel better when we view the dead. The dead don't care what they look like, the living care and Leo did look like he was sleeping—it still seemed unnatural. There would be no way he would be sleeping at a gathering of people nor would he ever be quiet.

There was soft music playing, very typical of what you would expect in a funeral home. It would have been more memorable of Leo if they had piped in the Yankees game which was on that evening. Leo was a big Yankees fan, I bet he was pissed he was missing the game that night. He told me once the only disappointment he had about his son was that he was a Mets fan; he called him "a traitor."

I was reflecting on Leo, wakes, music and the Yankees when Jaime made her entrance. She had tears streaming down her face. My first thought was doesn't she have a tissue? She first went over to Fran who was saving a seat for her. She sat down next to her, kissing her cheek and clasping her hands into hers. She then moved to Angelina kissing her as well; then to Tom shaking hands with him; then me, also shaking my hands saying, "Sorry for your loss." Then she moved to Rocky who stood up, and she wrapped her arms around him and began to sob loudly. I wonder what she would think if she knew Leo always referred to her as "the chubby ex-girlfriend of Rocky's." Maybe Leo only said that for my benefit. Leo was not a formally educated man but if there is an IQ for emotional intelligence his score would have been off the charts. He had been extremely adept at assessing people's emotions, using it to be kind or mean depending on his feelings for the person.

Jaime sobbed loudly for five minutes nonstop. Five minutes may not sound long but when you are listening to it without a break it can seem interminable. Anyone looking at Rocky and Jaime would think it was her father who had died. I tried very hard myself to hold my emotions in, fighting back tears, because this was not about me. I did mourn Leo but he was Fran's husband and Rocky and Angelina's father. They were the ones who should be comforted the most; not me or certainly not Jaime. But she did finally recover enough to return to her seat next to Fran, and gratefully, the "chubby ex-girlfriend" was quiet for the rest of the evening.

After the funeral mass at the cemetery the next day, Angelina told everyone at the gravesite they were invited to go to the house for brunch; some of Fran's friends had prepared refreshments for the gathering. I saw all these people milling about at the brunch, many of them not well known to Leo and others he didn't even like; all I could think of was how Leo was probably turning over in his grave because these people were in his house.

2019

Sixteen years ago George offered me a full-time gig singing with his band. Now history repeated itself and my emotional responses had not changed. Again, I was elated by the prospect but also sad because I obviously could not accept his offer now, sixteen years later. So I am not sure why I didn't reply immediately to his email: "Thanks so much, you don't know how much I would like to say yes George, but I can't move to Las Vegas because I am married with kids in high school." Instead, I told him I'd get back to him and like last time, I wanted to tell somebody about his offer—I needed to share my elation with someone.

I decided to tell Mattie. I knew he would think it was "awesome," because he loved hearing about my yearly jaunts to Vegas. He plays saxophone in a jazz band at his high school and begged me last year to take him to Vegas with me. He wanted to play in the band during the week I worked. I told him that he could come with me but I was not getting involved, it would be between him and George.

When the boys got home from school I thought Miles was Mattie at first glance. All those years I deliberately tried to dress them differently so they would not always be identified as "the twins," now they chose to dress exactly the same. They told me they liked to play jokes on teachers and girls who couldn't tell them apart. It made me laugh at the irony but at least it was their choice now, not mine.

As expected, Mattie was as thrilled as I was about George's job offer, but what started out as a shared imagining of—what if—as well as a bonding with my son ended badly. If he had simply said I should take the job everything would have been fine, but unfortunately he felt moved to elaborate more to encourage me to accept George's offer.

"Take it Mom, Dad wouldn't care if you left. He cheats on you all the time and Miles thinks so too."

It felt like I took a long time to respond, but in reality it only took seconds to turn into Medea willing to sacrifice my own son because he spoke of his father's betrayal. Medea knew that Jason cheated on her according to my Greek classics teacher in college. I didn't even know for sure Rocky had ever cheated on me. Never knew for sure, but all of that stored anxiety, fear, and anger that had been growing over the years nonetheless, got displaced and directed at Mattie that day instead of me confronting Rocky with my doubts and suspicions. And why was I so vehemently defending Rocky when I had suspected him of being unfaithful myself for our entire relationship? Was I really defending him or was it more about my own ego and self-esteem? Wasn't I really defending myself? If what Mattie said was true, it would also be true Rocky didn't care about me. I would have to admit that I was not valued in Rocky's eyes. I came to realize that day my reaction to Mattie was more about protecting my own fragile ego and less about defending Rocky. That was why I lashed out at my son.

I cared about myself more than I cared about my son, but having children is a selfish act in itself; it has always been a selfish act. It has never been about the children and I started to create imaginative fodder to excuse myself from being a bad mother. I might not win an award for Mother of the Year but my college sociology professor might have been proud. My thesis—the essential nature of selfishness in procreation. It could be supported with examples from the history of humans looking first at the paleolithic age, when having children was a means of protection. It was safer for early humans to be in groups; our species needed more numbers to survive. Then through the centuries beyond we needed more people simply to satisfy a need for more workers. Long before there was a concept of childhood, for centuries children were thought of as little grownups. In the modern world we do not need more people for safety or to satisfy the need for workers. Women have children today to give meaning to their lives, or because their girlfriends are having babies, or as in my case— we think of our babies as little miniatures of our loved one. Even if my thesis could be backed up—it did not justify my behavior towards Mattie.

Mitzy said if you love someone you would be willing to die for them. I would hope that I could run into a burning building to rescue my loved ones. What if I could only rescue one, who would I rescue? How would I choose between Miles or Mattie? Or would I need to rescue Rocky? It would be a selfish act rather than an heroic one if I chose Rocky over my children because of my need for him. When Leo died my mother said people crying at funerals were crying for themselves, not for the one who died. Rescuing Rocky would definitely be more about me than him. Philosophical ruminations didn't play through my mind at the time though only adrenaline feeding a fight response. Mattie did not assume a symmetrical stance. I was very ashamed of myself and proud of him in retrospect; he acted beyond his years.

"Well, just think about it, Mom."

The next day I tried to make it up to Mattie by giving him money to go to the movies with his friends and letting him play video games beyond the usual cut off time. I did apologize to him too for getting so angry with him, but I just had to add that he shouldn't be talking badly about his dad. I could not just leave it be; he responded with, "Whatever, Mom."

♪ ♫ ♩ ♪ ♫ ♩ ♪ ♫ ♩

Three days after receiving the email from George I still hadn't responded to him with my decision, my mind was totally on Rocky. He informed me that he had been talking to a woman he met, and he wasn't sure he wanted to remain married to me anymore. He'd have to think about it. What in hell did he mean he was talking to another woman? For our entire relationship, I always feared he would decide to go back to Jaime, so who was this woman?

Fran still talks about Jaime all the time, and Jaime still visits Fran on the weekends when she is with Angelina. Fran no longer recognizes her; the only reason I know that is because Angelina told me. I think Angelina felt better sharing that. It makes her feel like she's not the only one her mother doesn't recognize. But Angelina talking about Jaime did not conjure up a forgotten memory or fear for me. Jaime's presence is never far from my thoughts, she has always felt like a threat to my marriage for the past sixteen years. So, who is this other woman?

And why is Rocky giving me a warning about her? I told him years ago if he wanted to get out of this marriage to just tell me—I did not ask for foreshadowing. Also, what did he mean he had to think about it? Was I supposed to wait until he made a decision; didn't I have a say in this, too? Of course I did, and if I had still been in contact with Mitzy she would say, "What do you want Liz?" The problem was it didn't seem to be up to me anyway. I knew I wanted him and our marriage, but it was Rocky who had to think about it—because he had been talking with Dottie the dispatcher.

I couldn't stop thinking about how this was all wrong. It was supposed to be Jaime not Dottie the dispatcher. I wondered how Jamie would feel if he left me for Dottie instead of her. I was pretty confident she would be quite upset. That provided me with some perverse satisfaction in spite of my own pain. What were Rocky and the dispatcher talking about anyway? He had been off road patrol for years; the crashes had really gotten to him. He would tell me the horrific details and I knew it helped him to get the images out of his head, so I never shouted, "No, please don't tell me." I will forever see the images in my head until my dying day of the crash where the woman's head was decapitated, or another where Rocky had to pick up body parts scattered on the highway. When the crash happened on the Garden State Parkway, where the car caught on fire with the trapped little girl, and Rocky could not get to it in time to save her, he absolutely did not want to do road patrol anymore. He worked very hard for promotions that would remove him from the road, opting for a desk job with more pay to boot until retirement. Was he sharing war stories with Dottie while she gave him the details of today's road disasters? Did he still have a need to talk about his memories, and was she a comfort to him, replacing me?

He dropped this bomb on me late Friday afternoon during my meditative time. I was very mellow; sad to say I was still pretty depleted from my outburst at Mattie the other day as well, so my reaction to Rocky's announcement was very subdued. Truth be told, I never had screaming fights with Rocky during our entire relationship. I don't remember what I said to him when he told me about Dottie other than, "Who is she?"

When Rocky left the house shortly after, I began to sob. I out did Jaime's sobbing years ago at Leo's wake; I cried for longer than five minutes, more like twelve hours. I cried so hard and long that my eyes became raw and itchy until finally I didn't have any more tears left in me to cry. I put money on the kitchen table with a note telling the boys I wasn't feeling well and to order a pizza. I then retreated to the spare bedroom upstairs; it used to be their bedroom but they no longer used it since moving to the attic bedroom when they started high school. There was no way I was going to my bedroom; I didn't want to see or be near Rocky when he returned. I never thought we would need five bedrooms when Rocky bought this house but they would all be in use today. I laid down on the bed with my water bottle, a package of nuts that I didn't have an appetite for and listened to Billie Holliday. When Tam and Fran got home, I wondered why Tam did not knock on the door to ask me if everything was alright. Maybe she didn't even hear me with the music, but then she was hired to be my mother-in-law's caretaker, not mine. By the time Mattie knocked on the door to ask me if I was okay, I was no longer making audible sounds to accompany my tears; later, when Miles asked me if I wanted pizza I was on intermittent wipe. I told him no, the thought of pizza made me want to vomit. I stayed in the spare bedroom all night, hearing Rocky return about 2 am in the morning.

When I woke up the next day I was surprised to see it was 10 am. I had slept late, and I was famished since I hadn't eaten anything but the package of nuts since noon the previous day. I got up and went into the kitchen—the boys had left a note saying they hoped I felt better and that they went to the boardwalk with their skateboards. I was very impressed by this thoughtfulness coming from sixteen year old boys. I also noticed Rocky wasn't there but there was no note from him. I looked out the window, but only saw Tam and Fran in the backyard on the swing. After I ate I busied myself with doing the long neglected laundry. I was okay, or as okay as any woman could be, after her husband just told her he wasn't sure if he wanted to stay married to her. As long as I stayed busy I could distract myself, and thank goodness I was no longer crying. I don't think I had any more tears left anyway, and I decided to move back into my bedroom that evening. We had a queen size bed—I could keep away from Rocky—who more than likely would come home late again since it wasn't a work day for him tomorrow. There was no way I was sleeping in that uncomfortable single bed another night. I was surprised I had slept as well as I had; if Rocky didn't like it he could go sleep in Dottie the dispatcher's bed. He was no longer going to be my inspiration for singing *Since I Fell for You*. I wasn't leaving my bedroom again.

♪ ♫ ♩ ♪ ♫ ♩ ♪ ♫ ♩

It has been three weeks since Rocky dropped the bomb and he hasn't mentioned it since. In fact, when he came into the kitchen last night he patted me on the ass. Is he trying to pretend it never happened or trying to gaslight me? Maybe he had seen the email from George and fabricated this whole story about Dottie the dispatcher as a way of getting back at me. But it doesn't matter why he told me, there is no way I will allow this to be swept under the rug. We don't have any rugs after sixteen years living in this minimally furnished house anyway. I am not allowing Rocky to orchestrate the outcome of our estrangement—I am going to take control myself.

Some might ask why bother? Just leave him, he's a cheat. I guess Mattie and Miles feel that way. "Out of the mouths of babes comes truth." I heard my father say that but I also have heard or read "strength" or "wisdom" used instead of "truth" from other people or readings. I'll credit the boys for the truth perhaps, and Mattie for the strength to say it to me, but question their wisdom at sixteen years old. Truth, strength and wisdom are not synonyms—you cannot arbitrarily choose one of them to send the same message. Wisdom is your ability to judge what to do with your truth and strength. I also lied and deceived Rocky for years too. Maybe my kids would feel differently about me if they knew that. Many people might say my deception and Rocky's wasn't the same, but I think Mitzy had seen little difference between them. That may have been one of many reasons why it got to the point where she didn't want to be friends with me anymore.

Truthfully, his cheating would never be a reason for me to leave him. Imagining the exchange of body fluids never bothered me; it is the thought of intimacy that does. Perhaps that is what the injured party really means when they ask, "Do you love this person?" It's like what Mitzy said, love and lust can be confused, and I agree with her. Maybe I was in lust not in love with Rocky in the beginning. The love didn't come until there was intimacy. I remember feeling great love for him when he trusted me, feeling safe enough to be vulnerable—crying in my arms— it had nothing to do with sex. It's a pity I never gave Rocky the chance to comfort me because I was always too scared to let my guard down.

I do cheat with men too. Four of them: George, Julius, Tony and Rick. Not for sex, but we share intimacy when we play together. Making music that brings so much joy to each of us it rivals any love affair.

Sometimes I ask myself: have I focused too much on Rocky's negatives, and not enough on the positives, resulting from singing so many blues songs since I was sixteen years old? You never hear how good life is in the blues; if you did it wouldn't be the blues.

George is always saying you shouldn't overthink a song too much. If you do it can block you—you will not be able to sing. I am going to stop overthinking my relationship with Rocky. Tonight after dinner I am going to confront him. I am going to tell him I love him and I want our marriage, and ask him if he wants me and this marriage too. He gets no more time to think about it—time has run out. I don't anticipate crying, but it all depends on how I feel, what he says, and what happens. The only thing I know for sure is that I will not hide my emotions or vulnerability.

I need to settle my thoughts, it is my afternoon meditative time. I get a cup of tea and choose one of my favorite CD's to listen to—all the tracks are women jazz singers. I am just settling down when I hear Fran calling for Leo. Lately, she has become very agitated looking for him and it can take Tam a long time to calm her down. One thing I can say about Leo, I doubt he ever thought about cheating on Fran. There were a number of people who disliked him: they thought he was combative or a loudmouth. But he was devoted to Fran, he always called her "baby face." It has been a long time since her face has been that smooth. But maybe that's what he always saw when he looked at her—his high school sweetheart who he married immediately after graduation.

Ella Fitzgerald is just finishing *But Not for Me* when I no longer hear Fran and I see the packages on the piano seat. There are two of them wrapped in metallic blue gift wrap and the first thing I think is that they are from Rocky. I open up the first one and it is a book of sheet music, *Jazz Songs for Sopranos*. It's from Mattie and he wrote on the inside cover:

Don't give up your dream, Mom!

Margaret Whiting sang until she was 85.

Love Mattie

I guess some would be surprised that a sixteen year old boy in 2019 would even know who Margaret Whiting was, but he has been hearing me playing her songs as well as singing them since he was a baby. I once recorded myself singing *They Can't Take That Away from Me* and Mattie was trying to sing along with me. After we finished he said, "Is that good, Mommy?" in that voice of very young children when you can't tell whether it is a little boy or a little girl. I look at the song selections on the next page, and sure enough there it is, and Mattie put a star by it.

The second package is from Miles and it's a Rand McNally map of Las Vegas, and a bunch of papers he downloaded and printed from a web site called "The Best Magnet High Schools in Las Vegas," with a post-it saying:

Read This !!!

Love, Miles

I put the sheet music on the piano stand and the map and printouts in the piano seat. I gather all the wrapping paper and toss it in the kitchen trash. My tea is now cold so I make a fresh cup. By the time I return to my seat to once again try to settle down, Vanessa Rubin is singing *Black Coffee*. Great timing; I'm drinking tea but close enough.

Before I try to clear my mind, I mentally make promises to Mattie and Miles. To Mattie—I will not give up my dream. I might not have a voice kissed by angels, as my mother is so fond of saying when she is critiquing singers; and maybe my drive was more driven by a darker side for many years, but I refuse to stray from my course. To Miles, I promise that "I will read it."

But does he have any idea how hot summers can be in Vegas? Like me, Miles can't take the heat.

ABOUT THE AUTHOR

MARJORIE DURYEA has worked as an actress, director, choreographer and educator, teaching dance and communication on the college level. She is a member of SAG/AFTRA and AEA and holds a masters from Monmouth University in Communication. She is the author of two other novels-The Marriage Formula, Dead Cat in the Cupboard and the non fiction book, Diary of a Performing Arts Teacher. She lives at the Jersey Shore.

www.marjorieduryea.com.